SLAYGROUND!

The Omega defense computer sent messages to all parts of Wonderworld. Emergency traps were triggered. The Safest Place on Earth became the deadliest:

A herd of robot unicorns stampeded down on the agents. Some men died beneath the thundering hooves, while others were gored horribly.

In Pioneerland, a hail of arrows rained down. In Spaceland, small green Martians fired laser blasts. And the carnage in Joyland, the adults-only section of the park, was absolutely unspeakable . . .

PSI-MAN
Main Street D.O.A.

PSI-MAN

MAIN STREET D.O.A.
DAVID PETERS

DIAMOND BOOKS, NEW YORK

MAIN STREET D.O.A.

A Diamond Book / published by arrangement with
the author

PRINTING HISTORY
Diamond edition / April 1991

ISBN: 1-55773-492-5

Diamond Books are published by The Berkley Publishing Group,
200 Madison Avenue, New York, New York 10016.
The name "DIAMOND" and its logo
are trademarks belonging to Charter Communications, Inc.

PRINTED IN THE UNITED STATES OF AMERICA

10 9 8 7 6 5 4 3 2 1

Late November, 2021

1

THE SCREENING ROOM was darkened, and Terwilliger sat motionless, his fingers steepled, waiting for the sound of the creaking door that he knew would signal the arrival of The Man.

Terwilliger had come to enjoy these screenings, for it was the only time that The Man ever appeared the slightest bit discomfited. Ordinarily The Man was absolutely unflappable. Some claimed that his skin temperature was such that an ice cube left on his hand would not melt. The Man's face was unreadable, his thoughts unknowable.

But Lord above, did The Man hate the screenings.

Whenever Terwilliger met with The Man, a fine film of sweat seemed to spring magically into existence on the former's bald pate, onto which a few stray wisps of black hair still clung forlornly. It was at those times that he felt like a *Terwilliger*. Not like the magna cum laude graduate of Harvard Law School that he was; not like one of the highest positioned advisors in the "off-the-record cabinet"—not even like, as he indeed was, one of the most feared and whispered-about men in the government.

Nobody screwed with Terwilliger. Nobody. Because Terwilliger had his eyes and ears everywhere, and such was the governmental paranoia that one never knew if the most private conversation, anywhere from the boardroom to the bedroom, was being monitored or surveyed by Terwilliger. Whether it was being recorded by Terwilliger on the brand-new hard-disk technology that had just come leaping from the labs within the last few months. Whether, in fact, one's trusted working partner or even long-time lover might, in fact, be on Terwilliger's payroll.

This was the paranoia that Terwilliger preferred. But in the presence of The Man, this enjoyable position of power gave way to the basic insecurity he'd felt as a young man. Because his name—Arnold (or, God help him, Arnie) Terwilliger—just sounded so awful. So nebbish. So completely nowhere disgusting. Arnie Terwilliger wasn't the name of a power broker or life-in-the-fast-lane type of guy. It was a name that conjured up images of a low-level accountant, or the guy that the kids upended and tossed into trash cans, just for laughs.

Jake Powers. That was a name to reckon with. Or Zack Chase. Something like that. But Arnie Terwilliger? Christ, what a name to be saddled with. Unsurprisingly, he received little sympathy from his father, Arnold Terwilliger, Senior. His dad claimed that he'd passed the name on to his son because he was trying to develop a proud family tradition. Junior privately figured that it was simply a case of misery loving company.

It might seem odd, then, for a man to become a total control freak simply to make sure that his name was feared in all quarters rather than laughed at. Certainly Terwilliger Senior, a low-level accountant (naturally) wasn't that way. But Junior was.

Terwilliger had had a way about him, a drive, and a mind that was capable of ruthlessly analyzing a situation and finding the most expeditious course of action.

He remembered the Bill of Rights. He had been a youth at the time they'd been dismantled, and had been overjoyed. The damned things had been getting in the way. And at the advent of the Cards—those all-purpose means of identification and transaction—he'd been positively ecstatic.

Control, as he had written in a sixth-grade social studies analysis, *Control is everything*. It had been a paper so comprehensive and frightening that his teacher had asked Arnie's parents to come in for a conference. Arnie had intercepted the note, and a computer program he'd developed called his teacher for him, putting across such a convincing impression of his father (and being downright abusive, to boot) that teachers had steered clear of his parents ever since.

Which was fine with Arnie. The better to be in control.

He had worked his way up through the ranks of politicians, carefully analyzing who was going to be where, and who was likely to shoot to the top—the very top, because nothing else would do for Arnie Terwilliger. Arnie did not want to be president, because the president was not really in control. After all, there were all those other politicians all over you. Not to mention, of course, the public eye, which had a permanent blinder on it but nevertheless could prove something of an annoyance. And presidents, of course, were nominally obligated to uphold the Constitution, such as it was.

So the obvious thing was not to be the president, but the man who controlled the president. Which was what Arnie Terwilliger was.

He remembered when he had first met the president. He wasn't the president then, of course. No, he was a hard-driving senator who had *White House* written all over him. Terwilliger had analyzed the directions that the currents of history would be taking, and correctly surmised that this particular senator would be swept into power based on his track record, his drive, and the fundamental stupidity of the American voting public. Arnie had wrangled his way onto the senator's staff and had quickly impressed him with his brilliant and incisive comprehension of world affairs and how to take charge of them. It had been Arnie who had dubbed him "The Man," and it had stuck. The Man soon became a force to reckon with, his stature growing. And as that stature grew, so too did he cast that much greater of a shadow. Within that shadow, Terwilliger found a large, comfortable place to hide.

Election had been inevitable. Once in office, Terwilliger had preferred to remain in the cool comfort of the shadows, there to plan and manipulate. His role model was J. Edgar Hoover. Hoover had watched presidents come and go, and yet had stayed serenely in place. No one wanted to muck with him, because he knew too much. He knew where the skeletons were buried. Terwilliger was determined to know where the skeletons were buried too, even if he had to plant them there himself.

He was going to outlast The Man. No crummy limited terms for him. He was going to build his power base, increase his subtle influence, and become the guy who the public never heard of and the government feared. The president was The Man. Terwilliger was THE MAN.

Except when he was in the presence of the president. Because the president was an even bigger control freak than Terwilliger. Moreover, the president was an aggressive-enough personality that he wouldn't necessarily care that Terwilliger knew the whereabouts of the skeletons. If he was of a mind to, the president might simply plant Terwilliger along with the rest of them. It was a cautious chess game that Terwilliger played—to build his own power base without stepping on any presidential toes. The president was his greatest ally and also his greatest opponent.

So it was with some degree of joy that Terwilliger would attend these screenings with the president. Because it was at these screenings that the president let just a bit of his humanity show through, in the form of the discomfiture he felt in the presence of—

—the duck.

The door to the screening room creaked open. Terwilliger did not turn as he heard the president's heavy footfall. Instead he stared resolutely at the screen, as if watching a film already in progress. Moments later the president, *The Man*, sat down next to him.

He was ever so slightly out of breath, and Terwilliger said softly, "Just came from the gym, sir?"

The president nodded, running fingers through his shock of white hair. "Needed the workout," he said. "You could use one too, Arnie. Put some meat on that skinny frame of yours."

"Yes, sir," said Terwilliger differentially. "Are you ready to screen it?"

"Another one of those damned duck cartoons?" snapped the president.

"Yes, sir."

The president drummed impatiently on the armrest. "The last one was pretty damned insulting," he said sharply. "What did Wonder think he was doing, anyway? Did he think I wouldn't notice that vicious parody of my wife?"

"I don't know what Mr. Wonder was thinking," said Terwilliger. "I would assume he thought that it was funny."

"What Wyatt Wonder thinks is funny is of no interest to me," the president replied sharply. "Have you screened this one yet?"

"No, sir. I feel it best to form my opinions the same time as you do." Terwilliger had, of course, watched it the day before.

"Okay. Run it," said the president.

"Run it!" Terwilliger called out.

In the darkened room the screen seemed to spring to life.

The technology was nothing new. The multiplane technique used in the animation had long been in use for flight simulators, not to mention a ride in Wonderland entitled "Cosmic Express," which gave passengers the feeling that they were diving down into the heart of a supernova. But Wyatt Wonder had been the first to start using the technique for animation, and the resulting "Wonderflicks," as they had become known, revolutionized the animation industry. That was consistent. Whenever the animation field was revolutionized, as seemed to happen every decade or so, it was Wonder who was behind it.

The credits leaped onto the screen, big as life, almost threatening to envelop the room: *A MOBY DUCK CARTOON*. And sure enough, there was the lovable Moby himself. His sad-looking face with the trademark tuft of purple feathers atop his head.

Terwilliger risked a glance over at the president. The president wasn't moving, but he was glaring—glaring!—at the stupid duck. The duck looked back at him blandly and forced half a smile as if it could actually see the president and was trying to ingratiate itself to him somehow.

The scene shifted and suddenly they were on a waterfront. As was usual with the multiplane technique, there was a remarkable feeling of depth. The dock seemed to run off into the distance, and water lapping at either side was so realistic that one wanted to glance to the right or left to see if the ocean was intruding into the screening room. Lots of heavily muscled animated dockworkers were busy hauling crates, running forklifts, and the like.

A foreman, who they could only see from the back, stepped onto the screen and demanded to know where the new guy was. And sure enough, leaping onto the screen was America's favorite fowl, Moby Duck. Moby was wearing his trademark blue overalls and a watch cap pulled down that half covered his eyes. Moby, as he always was at the start of these cartoons, was incredibly skinny—a pathetic depiction of duckhood in general. He was slobberingly eager to please, and he saluted smartly to the new boss. "Yes, SIR! Anything you say, SIR!"

Terwilliger waited for it.

The camera reversed angle and the face of the foreman roared into view. The face was a caricature, the body distorted, with arms so long that they hung, gorillalike, to the ground. But the inspiration for the foreman was unmistakable. Not only was he unmistakable, but he was sitting in the room next to Terwilliger.

The president's body stiffened, his jaw set tightly, and Terwilliger was certain that he would order the film stopped. To his credit, however, he didn't.

He watched.

Moby Duck went through his cartoon paces, screwing up on a bigger and bigger scale. He would be crushed under falling crates, caught up in cargo nets, mashed, crunched, destroyed, and reconstituted in rapid succession. And all the time that bellowing, belligerent foreman would be haranguing him. The foreman who bore an unmistakable resemblance to The Man, right down to an occasional faint lisp that surfaced every now and then. The lisp was barely noticeable—except to a bastard like Wyatt Wonder, whose eye for parody never missed a thing.

And then the point was reached, as it always was in a Moby Duck cartoon. The affable fowl (who had just been dropped from a incomprehensible height after one of his "buddies" transfixed him with a cargo hook) was pushed beyond his capacity for politeness. And, as always happened in a Moby Duck cartoon, he "ducked out." What happened when Moby "ducked out"—a transformation that was aped by most seven- and eight-year-olds (and even, secretly, by their parents sometimes)—was that Moby would quite simply go—as he put it—quackers. His upper torso would swell to hilarious proportions, his arms would become impossibly muscled, his purple feathers would stand up straight (which many psychologists jumped all over as being clearly sexual in symbolism) and energized by this tremendous additional strength—the source of which was never clear—Moby would proceed to beat the living crap out of his tormentors. Be they one or a hundred, whoever had been bothering the poor duck throughout the preceding six minutes would suffer horribly during the last thirty seconds of frenzied, furious action.

Moby ripped into the other dockworkers, inflicting upon them all manner of cartoon mayhem. Pure, basic slapstick, and Terwilliger was careful not to laugh out loud. That was why, indeed, he had taken the precaution of watching the film the previous day. Moby Duck, in his beserker rage, tossed forklifts around as if they were poker chips. He tied one dockworker into knots, smashed another against a ship as if christening it, simply leveled everyone and everything that stood in his path.

And then he got to the foreman.

The president braced himself, as if preparing himself for the impact from the animated character.

"You're fired!" howled the foreman. Moby Duck, in response, hit him so hard that his head spun around about a dozen times, twisting his neck into a corkscrew. Moby grabbed the foreman's head, holding it stationary, and the rest of his body spun like a propeller. With this added momentum, Moby hurled him skyward, shouting his catch phrase, "You can't fire me! I quit!"

The foreman arced through the sky like a guided missile, his body still spinning and giving him momentum. His scream cut through the air as he shot above the clouds and then started to descend.

Seconds later his destination became evident. It was the White House.

"That son of a bitch," muttered the president as he watched his alter ego fall at ear-cracking speed, plunge through the roof of the White House, smash through floor after floor, before landing in the chair behind his desk of the familiar Oval Office. But the foreman hit the chair with such impact that it catapulted him forward, smashing through the wall and leaving an outline of himself behind. The president actually flinched at the impact, so much dimension did the multiplane give it.

And then, through the outline, Moby Duck stepped, now back in his skinny, nebbish, and lovable form. Moby sauntered across the Oval Office, vaulted the desk, and landed in the chair. He put his hands behind his head, his feet up on the desk, and sighed contentedly. "Nice office," he said in that annoying duck voice of his, and the cartoon faded out.

The president sat there for some time, unmoving, even after the lights came up. Terwilliger, taking his cue from The Man, made no move either.

"He's out of his mind," said the president at last. "He's out of his fucking mind if he thinks I'm going to let that travesty into the theaters of this country."

Wisely, Terwilliger said nothing.

"Get me the phone," said the president tightly.

Moments later Terwilliger was standing there with the phone in his hand. "Ring him," said the president.

"It's seven A.M. on the West Coast," said Terwilliger. "He might not be in his office."

"He'll be there," replied the president. "The bastard knows I'll be watching the thing around now. He'll be sitting there waiting for the call, smirking. Ring him."

Terwilliger did so, and sure enough the phone was picked up on the third ring. "Yaaaassss?" came a low, familiar voice.

"The president would like to speak with you," said Terwilliger. He had never met Wonder, and he knew Wonder had never met him. But they knew each other's voices all too well.

"That a fact?"

Terwilliger did not reply, but instead simply handed the phone to the president. The Man took it and said sharply, "What the hell did you think you were doing?"

Terwilliger placed a small jack in his ear. It tied into the White House recording system, so he could hear every word that was being said and also make sure that it was all being recorded.

"I thought I was getting an early start on my working day until you phoned, Mr. President," he heard Wonder's voice.

"You know damned well what I mean, Wonder. That cartoon of yours is an insult."

"You mean 'Dock Duck'? What's wrong with it?"

"Don't play these games with me, Wonder. You'll lose. Now either change the look of that foreman, and change the ending of the cartoon, or forget about releasing it into theaters."

"Well, I don't think that's possible right now."

"Why the hell not?"

"Because it's already in theaters."

Terwilliger gasped. Even he was caught flat-footed. He had underestimated the pure audacity of Wyatt Wonder. The president, however, made no discernible response. Instead he was silent for some seconds, as if composing himself.

"Our understanding, Wonder," said the president carefully, "was that I screened every cartoon before it was released. You are now telling me that it's out in Wonder Theaters already?"

"All over the country," said Wonder, sounding surprisingly neutral (Terwilliger thought) considering that he was probably trying not to chortle too loudly. "I agreed to screen all our shorts and features for you, Mr. President. But I'm not certain what gave you the impression that I awaited approval before releasing them."

"I've requested changes in the past—"

"And I've made them whenever possible. That's courtesy. But courtesy isn't the same as servitude, Mr. President."

The Man was silent for some seconds more. "Recall it."

"Pardon?"

"Recall that odious cartoon immediately."

"No."

"No?" He was astounded. It was not a word the president was accustomed to hearing. "No what?"

"No, sir. Now, of course, if you want to try and go storming into Wonder Theaters and pull out the short, or even shut the theaters down—well, now, you're welcome to try. Of course, you remember what happened the last time you did that."

The president did indeed. It had been a feature-length film entitled *Cliffhangers*, and the president hadn't noticed the split-second subliminal message that said, "THE PRESIDENT SUCKS," dropped into the middle of the film. But *Cliffhangers* had proven so popular that riots had broken out where the government had tried to shut it down (once an eagle-eyed operative had noticed the message during a matinee). It had not been a pleasant scene, and the president did not want a repeat.

"So, Mr. President, if there's nothing else . . . see you in the funny papers." And with that, Wyatt Wonder hung up.

The president stared at the phone for a moment, and then passed it over to Terwilliger.

"I should have seen this coming," said the president with a sigh. "Wonder Films grew and grew, taking over everything, ruling the entertainment world—dammit, I should have headed it off somehow."

"There was nothing you could have done," said Terwilliger.

There was another silence, and Terwilliger knew what would be coming next.

"It would be a shame," said the president, "if something happened to Wyatt Wonder."

"Something temporary?"

"Something permanent. Very permanent. Something that would put that little weasel in a place where he couldn't do any harm—like a pine box six feet under!" His voice had grown louder, more belligerent with each word, and he had ended the sentence with his fist slamming on the armrest.

"Are you saying, Mr. President," asked Terwilliger very softly, "that we should arrange to have Wyatt Wonder—killed?"

The president looked at him with large, innocent eyes. "Of course not," he said. "That would be . . . wrong."

"Yes, sir."

"So we understand each other."

"Perfectly, sir. As always, perfectly."

And Arnie Terwilliger was in control once more.

2

THE JEEP HAD given its all, but finally the exhausted vehicle collapsed in Los Angeles. It did not pick an especially good place to do it, either, namely at a corner in one of the seamier parts of the city.

Chuck Simon tried to coax the engine into turning over one final time, but it didn't seem remotely interested in his prayers or pleadings. He turned the key again, and then again, but each time was rewarded with merely a sound that was like rusted gears crunching together, or a broken something rubbing against a busted something else. Chuck cursed his lack of knowledge of all things mechanical, even as he climbed out of the jeep. He went around to the front and lifted the hood, staring in hopeless dismay at the engine in front of him. He held a vague hope that somehow the engine would say to him, with infinite patience, "Look, idiot, here's what's wrong with me, over here. You can fix it. Any moron could fix it." The engine, for its part, remained frustratingly silent.

He heard a loud clearing of throats from nearby. Slowly he turned, knowing what he was going to see.

They stood a few feet away, a small gang of punks. In a way, Chuck almost felt sorry for them. These days, the simple act of staying alive was something of a challenge, and strength in numbers was a good way of increasing the odds. Unfortunately the numbers were stacked against them in this case.

"Yes?" Chuck asked politely. He stood, and his muscular build gave the silent message that, whatever they had in mind, he was not going to make it easy for them.

There were four of them, wearing the same red jackets. One of them was half turned, and Chuck noticed a picture of a crab stenciled on the back. It was probably their gang name.

An attack of the crabs. Wonderful. He'd have to remember to scrub thoroughly afterward.

Chuck's t-shirt was stretched tightly across his chest, and his jeans also fit snugly. His jacket lay in the jeep's front seat, because the weather was so irritatingly humid that he had no need for it. Los Angeles had always been known for its warm weather, but the permanent smog alert that the city labored under had kicked the average temperature in the city up two degrees every year for close to a decade now. It was not a pleasant place to be, and nobody much liked living there these days.

The black dye that Chuck had used to disguise his blond hair had long since grown out, and he hadn't kept it up. After all, those who were pursuing him would have been looking for a dark-haired man by now, so he had to change his appearance. He had trimmed the beard away and kept only a moustache that ran down either side of his mouth, Fu Manchu style. His piercing blue eyes studied the four young men narrowly. "Can I help you with something?" he asked.

"We want your Card," one of them said.

"That's a very popular request," said Chuck. He removed the plain white ID Card he kept in his hip pocket and flipped it to them. "Here," he said. "It's not mine. And the man I took it off of has probably been found dead by now, so it won't do any of you any good. But use it. Be my guest."

"How about if we shove it up your ass?" another one of them said.

Chuck sighed. "Whoa. You guys are too tough for me. I don't know if I can cope with the tough guys I keep running into. Like the guys back in Colorado. They were real tough. Wound up real dead too."

The four punks laughed at that, for Chuck was talking so softly, so calmly, that his manner was at total odds with the words he was speaking.

"We want the car then."

At that Chuck laughed out loud. "It's broken! You want to get it started, good luck."

"Can use a car for pieces, man," said one of the punks. They started toward the vehicle.

"Good luck then," said Chuck, stepping back. "Although—I forgot to mention it—if you want the thing, you'll have to take it up with my business partner."

"Oh, yeah," the leader sneered. "You got some pussy partner?"

"Not exactly," said Chuck. "More like a doggie."

There was a low growl from the back seat of the jeep. The punks who had been approaching stopped dead.

"A very big doggie," Chuck continued calmly.

Slowly the massive head of a German shepherd rose from hiding. He opened his mouth wide, yawning, and the mouth could have easily encompassed the head of anyone standing there.

"A very big doggie who was napping," Chuck added.

The dog drew his front up with his paws, leaning over the front seat. His head slowly swiveled in the direction of the punks, taking them in and licking his chops languorously.

A single word sounded inside Chuck's head.

Lunch?

Chuck turned to the punks who were standing there and said, "He wants to know if you're lunch. Are you?"

Their mouths moved but no words emerged.

"I think," said Chuck slowly, "that it would be in your best interests to convince him you're not, in fact, lunch—by getting out of here. Don't you fellows think that would be good?"

One of them started to make a motion for the back of his

jacket but Chuck said sharply, "I wouldn't do what you're thinking of doing." The punk froze, and Chuck went on, "He'll tear you to pieces before the gun clears the holster. And as much as I would hate to see it happen, you caught me at a really unhappy time. I've got a splitting headache, and this weather isn't helping my sinuses. So you're thinking of pitting your little gun and your reflexes against my associate's speed, his teeth, and my unpleasant mood. Add it all up, I think you're going to come out on the debit side. Is any of this getting through to you? Just nod. That's a boy," he said encouragingly as the punk nodded once. "Now back up, very slowly, and all of you just go on your way, and no one is going to have to end up as shreds of meat."

He watched as the four of them moved off, looking sullen and trying to act cocky to each other, to convince one another that none of them had really been the least bit nervous. Rommel looked at Chuck accusingly. *There goes lunch*, he said.

Chuck hadn't been lying. His sinuses really were killing him, and he still wasn't one hundred percent over his grueling ordeal in Colorado. And now the damned dog was pestering him about food. In anger, Chuck slammed down the hood and said, "You know, I'm getting a little sick of your single-mindedness. You're utterly obsessed with food."

When I'm hungry, I think about food.

"But you're always hungry!"

So I'm always thinking about food. So what's the problem? the dog retorted in his head. *It's not like I'm thinking about food when I'm not hungry.*

"But you're always hungry!" Chuck said again, waving his hands about agitatedly.

Then try giving me some food. Boy, you're slow today.

Chuck sighed in exasperation. "This is getting us nowhere."

I agree.

"So what would you suggest? No, don't say it," he cut

Rommel off before the inevitable request could be framed in his mind. "Come on."

Where are we going?

"Anywhere is better than here."

Chuck slung the backpack that had his few belongings in it and started to walk. Rommel hesitated a moment and then hopped out of the jeep after him. When the dog landed on the pavement, Chuck could have sworn that it shook a bit under him.

Rommel padded alongside him and said after a moment, *You don't know where we're going.*

"No, I don't." Chuck was walking quickly, fists clenched, trying to take in a decent breath. "Do you?"

Hey, you're the brains of this outfit.

"Well, someone has to be. And you're the stomach, I suppose."

Well, someone has to be.

Chuck sighed. Rommel did that all the time; threw his own words back at him. It got annoying after a while.

Suddenly Chuck stopped, a split second before Rommel did. His sinus problems were forgotten as something else screamed warnings at him.

Rommel sensed it too. Actually, he had detected the danger a split instant before Chuck, but had been just that much slower to react to it. His fur bristled and he growled low in his throat.

Slowly Chuck looked around, trying to pick up with his eyes what his mind had already warned him about.

None of the buildings around them were more than three stories tall, mostly residential although there was a fruit and vegetable stand, a small grocery store, and, oddly enough, a comic-book store called "Page After Page." The rest of the stores were boarded up, and had FOR RENT signs thick with dirt or graffiti. The traffic light was broken, and had not been attended to since maintenance crews disliked coming to this section of town. Besides, not many cars came through either. Indeed, the only reason Chuck was there was because he'd gotten off the freeway immediately upon hearing the beginning of his engine's demise.

There were no sounds. No sounds of radios blaring, or vids playing, or children playing some innocuous game in the streets. An old person was shuffling down the street, leaning on his cane. In the air was a generally acrid smell, and in patches the tar was melting so much that people walking over it left shoe prints.

Chuck looked up at the boarded-over windows above the shops. He saw alleyways nearby, leading in between narrow and decrepit buildings, cloaked heavily in shadows.

Everywhere, Rommel told him.

Chuck nodded slowly. "But not for me," he whispered.

No, or you'd be dead by now—or have noticed them earlier. What's happening?

"I don't know. And I'm sorry, since I'm the brains, I should. But I don't. Satisfied?" He was talking quickly, harshly, and softly, as if something was driving him to talk as fast as he could. As if this might be his last opportunity.

Then he heard the car.

Cars, actually. Two of them, and the reason that they stood out—aside from the general silence—was that their motors sounded like airplane engines, throbbing and powerful.

Chuck tensed, drifting in reverse so that his back was against one of the buildings. He looked left and right, his mind screaming at him now. Next to him, Rommel's growling grew louder, almost loud enough to drown out the car engines.

"Whoever's in the car," said Chuck.

They're the enemy.

"No," Chuck said, with sudden realization. "They're the target."

Wyatt Wonder studied the monitor, stroking his chin thoughtfully as the onboard camera made a slow sweep of the surrounding area. He leaned back in his seat, the one that had been custom-designed to accommodate the long legs that supported his six-six frame. His entire body was large-boned, but his head was contrastingly small. It diluted some of the menace that such a huge individual might ordinarily carry with him, perhaps even prompted people to underestimate him. He had high cheekbones and small eyes set under heavy eyebrows. His black hair was precisely trimmed, a perfect horizontal line across his forehead, and hanging just over the tops of his ears.

Across from him, seated next to the monitor screen, the man from the city offices—Jackson was his name—was talking eagerly, trying to remain cool while at the same time sharing his exuberance over the project they were discussing.

The limo they rode in rolled over a pothole, but the shock absorbers were such that the bump was barely felt inside.

"As you can see, Mr. Wonder," Jackson was saying, "this section of the city is prime for the type of project you've been discussing. Just say the word, sign the papers, and we can have crews out here by next week."

"Demolishing the place." When Wonder spoke it was in a low, thoughtful rumble, as if his mind were elsewhere.

"That's right."

"And the people?"

Jackson shrugged indifferently. "A lot of squatters, a few Cardless wonders. Few people with any legal claim to being here. And the handful who do could be persuaded."

Wonder sat back, studying the screen with its slowly moving image. "I don't want to see this development created atop the bodies of innocent people," he said.

"Well . . . well, none of us does, certainly," Jackson said quickly, smiling as best he could.

"Bringing life to downtown L.A. is something we all want to see happen," Wonder continued, as if he hadn't even heard Jackson speak. "The building of Wonder Estates could go a long way toward that."

"A place where people could live and feel safe," intoned Jackson.

"Just like Wonderworld," said Wonder. "People go to Wonderworld because they want to feel safe for a few hours. They want to be able to leave their problems at the gate and know that when they're in Wonderworld, they're safe from the pinheads, the zipheads, the freaks, and the

Snappers. How great it would be if their home lives could be like that too."

"I absolutely agree, Mr. Wonder."

Wonder stroked his chin thoughtfully. "It would be fabulous, wouldn't it?"

"Yes it would, sir."

"Just a handful of squatters, you said?"

"Yes, sir."

Wonder shrugged expansively. "Screw it, then. Get out the ones who have no right to be there. Grease the palms of the ones who are reluctant. If that goes smoothly, we can do some serious business."

Jackson's head bobbed up and down excitedly. "Then I can tell the mayor's office that it's a go."

"You can tell him that once you've done as I asked, then we can proceed. Until that time I sign nothing, dispense nothing, spend nothing. Connie, are you getting all this down?"

Connie was seated next to Wonder, and had been briskly tapping the keys on a portable word recorder. Jackson glanced at her again, as he had been doing surreptitiously the entire ride. She was a striking young woman, Mexican by the look of her. She had long brown hair and a pleasant oval face. Her tanned legs were crossed in a no-nonsense fashion, the recorder carefully balanced on her lap.

"Mr. Wonder, with all respect to the young lady"—and Jackson gestured toward Connie—"why didn't you just have a recording device taking down this meeting?"

"Chalk it up to eccentricity." Wonder smiled mirthlessly.

Jackson didn't pursue it, but instead said, "Mr. Wonder, you're asking the mayor's office—the city—to undertake a fairly large-scale house-cleaning operation, and refusing to put up any sort of commitment of your own. I don't know if we can do that."

"Then return to your masters and find out if you can. I'm in no hurry, Mr. Jackson. I have all the time in the world."

But as he spoke he was leaning forward and staring at the monitor. The camera had been doing steady 360-degree turns and was now focused behind them. A garbage truck was now following them and Wonder frowned. "I thought you said city services didn't like to get down here all that often."

"They don't," affirmed Jackson, puzzled.

"Remarkable coincidence that a garbage truck would show up just now, don't you think?"

That was the moment when the explosion rocked the car.

The car swerved wildly, tires screeching, and Connie screamed once as she was thrown against her employer. Jackson likewise cried out, but Wonder's mouth was set firmly in a thin line.

"What's happening?" screamed Jackson.

"Reviews are in on the latest Moby Duck short," replied Wonder tersely.

Chuck and Rommel watched as the two black stretch limousines turned the corner and started down the street. Chuck was looking all around, his head throbbing with warning—

And the old man with the cane across the street suddenly stood up, no longer looking the least bit lame. He shouldered his cane, aimed, and fired at the lead car.

High-impact shells leaped from the cane and smashed into the side of the lead car. The car skidded, its side caved in but still intact, a mute testimony to its heavy armor plating. The old man fired again, and this time the side of the lead car was blown out completely. The car flipped over, gas tank rupturing. Gasoline poured out onto the street, spewing out in all directions.

The car behind had slammed to a halt and started to back up. But the garbage truck had pulled up behind them, bringing its bulk lengthwise and cutting off their retreat.

From the lead car, armed men were trying to pull themselves out. Two were visible, covered with blood, although it was uncertain whether it was their own or one of their fellows, still unseen.

Chuck looked around desperately, not sure where to react or what to do. Everything was happening far too quickly.

The trickle of gasoline had reached the old man—who

obviously wasn't so old—and he flipped a lighted match onto it. As if jet-propelled, a path of flame leaped into existence and shot toward the overturned car.

The men struggling to get out had only an instant to realize what was about to happen before the flame trail reached the breached gas tank. Chuck saw it too, saw he only had an instant, and reached out with his mind. The two visible men were yanked from the car as if pulled by invisible strings, hurled across the street just before the flame trail reached the helpless auto.

Chuck saw another arm emerge from the side window of the car, too late. The flame got to the gas tank and an instant later the car exploded. Chuck buried his face in Rommel's hide as the air sizzled around him. He heard a *shuck* sound and looked up to see a large piece of metal embedded in the wall a few inches above his head.

"We've got to do something!" hissed Chuck.

Yeah. Not get killed.

"Besides that!"

There is nothing besides that.

"Yes there is!"

You mean . . . lunch?

"You're impossible!"

The surviving limo was suddenly swinging around, its front now aimed at the old man. For a moment Chuck thought that it was going to run him over, but instead suddenly there was the sound of machine-gun fire. The origin was not evident at first, but then Chuck saw the old man hurled back against a building, his body dancing an insane jig. Then he slid to the ground, leaving a massive smear of blood behind him against the wall.

The car started to back up and then swung around. The garbage truck still prevented backing up, and the burning hulk of the lead car made forward motion impossible.

From directly overhead the boards over the windows were smashed out, wood raining down on them. Chuck did not need to see to know what was about to happen. Within seconds the air was filled with the steady sound of bullets flying, chewing up the street, strafing the car.

The car started to back up, despite the lumbering presence of the garbage truck, and then bullets blew out the right side tires.

Chuck looked around desperately and saw the only good thing about the situation—there were no guns set up on the opposite side of the street. They must have been concerned about possible crossfire.

The car windows were becoming a spiderweb of cracks, holding up under the barrage but just barely. Within seconds even the reinforced windows would shatter. The car roared forward, just dodging a missile that streaked from overhead, ripping up the street.

Chuck emerged from the alleyway and started running, hugging the edges of the building. No one paid any attention to him.

Where the hell are you going? Rommel demanded.

"I can't stand by and let this happen!"

Maybe whoever's in the car deserves this. Did that occur to you?

Suddenly the car door on the opposite side flew open and a bespectacled man, arms over his head, leaped out. He turned and screamed, "I'm Jackson! I'm with the mayor's office! I'm not part of—"

Whatever else he might have said was cut off by the bullets that strafed his chest. He flew back as if smashed by a giant fist, blood pouring from his open mouth, arms pinwheeling in an almost grotesquely comedic style. He fell to the ground, upper body chopped into pulped meat.

Just before the car door slammed shut, Chuck heard a woman's scream.

Great. A woman. "Chivalry is not dead," he muttered.

No, but you'll be, sounded in his head. Stupid dog.

He stayed in the shadows of the building and then, taking a deep breath, ran toward the garbage truck.

As he dashed across the street, he risked a glance at the ambushers in the third story. There were about a half-dozen men, all wearing jackets, all wearing sunglasses or some other sorts of eye shields.

Government men. He was certain of it. And there was

one guy, with what looked like some sort of rocket launcher perched on his shoulder, taking dead aim on the car.

It was a hell of a distance, even for Chuck, and he was in motion at the same time. Nevertheless his mind lashed out, trying to grab the launcher away. He put the full force of his TK against it.

He didn't succeed in pulling it away. What he did do, however, was literally shove the missile back in just as it launched.

The weapon exploded, taking with it the launcher, the man holding the launcher, the several men surrounding it, and the upper story of the building. There were screams, and a body plummeted from an upper window, afire and blazing like a comet. It hit the ground with a hideous sound.

Chuck's eyes widened in horror. Oh, God. He hadn't meant to do that. He had just wanted to stop it. It was happening again. God help him, it was happening again.

And another part of himself said no, this wasn't like that other time. This wasn't fury and unfettered revenge. This was trying to protect someone, and it hadn't been intentional.

Even as he tried to convince himself of that, he made it to the driver's side of the garbage truck.

Inside the car Connie was trying to keep herself under control as Wyatt Wonder scanned the area with his onboard camera, which was, miraculously, still working. The driver, with icy calm, was saying, "Still no way out, sir. And both right side tires are out. We wouldn't get far even if we could move."

"That man just cannot take a joke," said Wonder calmly.

"You . . . you let Jackson go out and get shot!" Connie said, lip quivering. She was trying to ignore the sounds of machine guns, tried not to look at the rapidly withering defense that the windows were providing them.

"He wanted to take his chances outside," replied Wonder. "His exact words, as I recall. People forget that chances don't always pan—"

At that moment came the explosion caused by the

jammed rocket launcher. Operating the camera manually, Wonder spun it around to view with amazement the conflagration at the top of the building. "What the hell—?" he said.

He turned the camera around, trying to determine the cause, and then spied a blond man dashing toward the garbage truck.

"What have we here?" Wonder said with preternatural calm.

Chuck got to the garbage truck door and yanked it open. The driver, dressed in the same anonymous "uniform" as the other gunmen, turned in surprise and had his handgun out, aimed right at Chuck.

Chuck's mind shoved the gun hand upward, the bullet exploding harmlessly over his head. Then his mind yanked forward, hauling the driver out of his seat.

The gun flew from his fingers and, to his credit, the gunman did not question what was happening but instead simply leaped at Chuck, hands outstretched. Chuck had no time for gentleness. He grabbed the man's outstretched arm, pivoted, and allowed his attacker's speed to carry him forward. Chuck followed through and slammed the gunman's head into the side of the garbage truck. Even as the gunman crumbled to the ground Chuck was leaping into the driver's seat.

"Rommel, come on!" he shouted.

The dog heard him, or heard his mind, and ran from hiding as the truck lunged forward. *I'd give my life to protect you, but this is really stupid,* Rommel informed him as he leaped up into the passenger seat.

"Thanks for the assessment. Hold on."

He saw out the side that men were emerging from the burning building. So he hadn't gotten all of them. Part of him was relieved—until he realized that they wouldn't exactly be grateful for what he had done.

The garbage truck hurtled forward and then slammed to a halt next to the unmoving limo, positioning itself between the limo and the assailants. Chuck was trying to think of a way to convince those inside that he was not out to hurt them when his work was done for him as the limo doors opened.

A huge man emerged, followed by the woman who Chuck presumed had done the screaming. The driver leaped out from the front door.

"In the back!" shouted Chuck as he started to drive the truck forward. He pointed madly behind him, since there was no room whatsoever in the cab.

It was a side-loading truck, and the three escapees leaped into the hopper area directly behind the cab. They ducked down, the wind-doors on either side protecting them from the initial flurry of bullets that hailed around them.

The truck stalled out.

The gunmen converged, and with an unaccustomed curse merged with a desperate prayer, Chuck put the truck in neutral and twisted the key. The engine miraculously turned over and Chuck slammed the truck into gear and hurtled forward. In front of him was the burning wreckage of the first car, but Chuck didn't slow down at all. He braced for the impact and shot through at full speed, flame and pieces of burning metal all around him. For a moment he felt as if he were driving into hell, and then suddenly he was through. From behind came the sounds of shots as the frustrated gunmen fired helplessly, bullets *pinging* off the sides of the heavy truck.

"Our passengers all right?" called out Chuck.

Rommel poked his head out and glanced around. *Look shaky, but okay.*

The truck sped through the streets, Chuck ignoring the streetlights in those instances where they went against him. He had no time to fool around, desperate to put as much distance between himself and the scene of the ambush as possible. Besides, he wasn't in a vehicle that was built for either speed or subtlety. If they were of a mind to follow him, it wouldn't exactly be difficult.

Suddenly a black limo was alongside them.

Chuck glanced down, saw that the driver was gesturing

madly. He wasn't sure of what to do. If this was a trick—

But then he glanced in his sideview mirror and saw that the tall man in the hopper was also gesturing, indicating that Chuck should pull over. On that urgent if somewhat nerve-wracking recommendation, Chuck slowed the truck down, angling toward the curb.

The limo pulled over as well and within moments Chuck's passengers had emptied out and jumped into the limo. All except for the tall man, though, who stood there and gestured that Chuck should come along with them.

"They'll be looking for you!" shouted the tall man. "You won't last five minutes. You need my protection!"

What's he saying? asked Rommel.

"That we need his protection."

Well, we need somebody's. Way things are going, you're going to get us killed, and I'll die on an empty stomach, and—

"All right, all right!" shouted Chuck, as much to Rommel as to the man. He jumped out of the cab and hit the street, Rommel right after him.

The tall man gasped. "That dog belong to you?"

"Lord knows no one else would want him."

Thanks.

"All right, come on," and he gestured toward the car. Rommel climbed in first and Chuck heard a startled shriek, indicating that Rommel had met the young woman.

"Lucky this limo of yours showed up."

"I radioed we were in trouble," replied the tall man. "Just a matter of time until we were tracked down." He gestured for Chuck to climb in, which Chuck did. Chuck was surprised, as the tall man got in, that considering he, the woman, the tall man, and Rommel were all in the back, it didn't seem very crowded.

"Who are you?" said the tall man as the limo pulled forward.

"I'm Chuck. This is Rommel," said Chuck, hoisting a thumb at the dog. Rommel seemed to be appraising the young woman.

"I'm Wyatt Wonder," said the tall man.

Chuck blinked. "Really?"

"Really. And, Chuck"—he clapped a massive hand on his shoulder—"I think we're going to be able to do some business together. Drink?"

3

THE OLD MAN laughed.

He sat in his chair—the one he never moved from—and watched the animated characters going through their antics. It was pure joyous amusement.

He chuckled and guffawed as Moby Duck went berserk, remembering the first time he'd come up with that gag, remembering how it had been almost accidental. That he'd been trying to come up with a consistent way to bring each cartoon to a climax in a way that audiences would anticipate, appreciate, and never grow tired of.

Ducking out. Going quackers. These had been the catch phrases he had developed. Him, the old man, and they'd worked their way into the language.

Moby was going up against his favorite antagonist, Pistol Pete. At the moment Pete was being shoved down a toilet. The kids loved that one.

So did the old man, because no matter how old he was, he was still a kid at heart.

He called out his son's name. "Wyatt? You here? You're missing the best part." But Wyatt wasn't there. Wyatt rarely was. Instead he was running around, playing with his friends.

Someday, thought the old man. *Someday Wyatt would settle down.* Maybe then he would even let him get involved with the company. But not now. Wyatt was just a kid. Kids should be happy-go-lucky and involved with their little friends, not a part of the cutthroat world of movie making. Making cartoons—that was grown-up's work.

The old man stopped calling for his son and settled back to watch the end of the cartoon.

The limo roared through the streets of Los Angeles and then up onto the freeway. Once there the speed picked up considerably.

"Wyatt Wonder," Chuck said, holding a soft drink carefully so as not to spill it. "I'll tell you, this is a major surprise for me. Believe it or not—I still have my original Wonder Club ring. Well, I did," he amended. "Not with me. It's back in . . . well, it's kind of complicated."

"Oh, it's a shame it's complicated," said Wyatt Wonder. "The Wonder philosophy is that everything is simple. Although I'll tell you this—you could get five hundred dollars for a Wonder Club ring in mint condition on the Wonderana market."

"Wonderana?"

"Collectibles. Memorabilia. That sort of thing. Collectors are very avid."

"Five hundred?" Chuck whistled.

When do we eat?

"Later," said Chuck.

Wonder looked at him curiously. "Later for what?"

"Nothing. Look, Mr. Wonder, this is all very interesting, and it's really an honor to meet you and all, but maybe you should just drop me off somewhere."

"Really?" Wyatt leaned back, carefully cradling a gin and tonic. "And why is that?"

"It just might be—"

From next to them, Connie shrieked. The men turned as Connie pointed accusingly at Rommel. "He stuck his nose between my legs."

She uses something down there, Rommel informed him.
I was curious about the scent.

"Keep your curiosity to yourself, Rommel," Chuck said
sharply. He looked apologetically at the embarrassed young
woman. "Sorry. He was checking out—well, he was—"
And to his surprise he felt his cheeks flushing. "It won't
happen again."

She actually smiled slightly at Chuck's obvious discomfiture. "Well . . . I mean, he's just a dumb animal, after
all."

You're not exactly genius level yourself, sweetheart.

Chuck cleared his throat to cover up a cough. Rommel
hadn't always been this perceptive of what humans were
saying. But lately he'd gotten better and better at it,
probably funneling his comprehension through Chuck's
mind. Just what Chuck always wanted to be. An interpreter
for a randy canine.

"I'm waiting for you to complete that sentence,
Mr. . . . ?"

Wonder's inquiry as to Chuck's surname hung in the air,
waiting for Chuck to complete it. "Jones," he said, fishing
the first simple name he could out of the air.

"Mr. Jones," continued Wonder calmly. "What do you
think will happen if you remain in our company?"

Chuck glanced around, his gaze lighting on Rommel.
Rommel stared at him passively, his great head on his
forepaws. "There are . . . certain individuals who would
be happier if I were . . . how do I put this . . . ?"

"Dead?" said Wonder helpfully.

"For starters," admitted Chuck.

"Well, Mr. Jones, as you can see, I am not exactly on the
approved list of certain gentlemen as well."

"It's hard to believe, Mr. Wonder, that whatever you
have yourself involved in, that you've offended people
higher positioned than the people I've offended."

Wonder took a sip of his drink. "The President of the
United States?"

Chuck stared at him openly. "You win," he admitted.

"I always win," said Wonder pleasantly. "The longer

you're with me, the sooner you'll realize that. So, Mr. Chuck Jones—"

He paused a moment and smiled, as if the name brought some sort of private amusement to him. "Chuck . . . I think it may be advantageous if you stayed with me for a time."

"Despite the danger I might present to you?"

"Thus far," said Wonder, "that danger merely exists in your claims of being pursued. As you have seen, those who would seem to be angered with me are very, very real. Which reminds me . . ." He put out a hand in a gesture that Connie was used to, and she reached over and handed him the car phone. "Are you sure you want to do this?" she asked him.

He looked at her quizzically. "Whyever not?" he asked. "Horace," he addressed the driver, "how long to Wonderworld?"

"Five minutes, Mr. Wonder," replied the driver briskly.

"That's what I thought. We'll be safe enough before he can do anything further. Phone . . . get me Goofy." Upon Chuck's confused look, Wonder said, "A private joke. My phone has various frequently called numbers pre-encoded, tied in to certain code names. Goofy, for example, dials directly . . . ah! Mr. President," he said cheerfully.

Chuck paled slightly at Wonder's cavalier tone. Connie said nothing, but her expression held more of an annoyed look than anything, as if she had heard this kind of thing many times before.

"Mr. President, I'm sorry to bother you," said Wonder, "but I just thought you should know that I ran into a bit of a problem. A great deal of shooting and all that. You wouldn't happen to know anything about that, would you?" He paused, then smiled at Chuck and gave a thumbs-up gesture. "Not a thing? Mr. President, are you quite all right? You sound ill. You know what the perfect cure for that is? One of my films. I suggest you kick back and enjoy one at your earliest convenience, and don't worry . . . if there isn't one you like now, there will be in the not-too-distant future. Take care now."

He disconnected and flipped the phone over to Connie. She shook her head disapprovingly. "Sooner or later he's going to get annoyed when you do that."

"He already got annoyed. Which brings us back to Chuck here. Chuck"—and Wonder slapped him on the knee—"how would you like to work for me? Ah. Here's our exit."

The limo angled downward off the highway, and Chuck was immediately struck by the change in the area now that they were outside of L.A. This area was filled with glittering lights, well-kept buildings, relaxed people walking the streets with balloons in their hands and smiles on their faces. It was certainly quite a contrast.

Several passersby actually seemed to recognize the limo and waved excitedly, even though they couldn't see the occupant through the reflective window. Wonder, for his part, waved absently and said briskly to the driver, "Horace . . . entrance C, I think. Entrance C?" he asked Connie, as if he needed her approval. She shrugged.

The limo hung a right, and then a left, and Chuck watched out the window. They were circling the perimeter of what seemed to be a huge armed camp. The walls were twenty feet high, glistening metal with gaily colored towers every hundred feet or so. Night had fallen, and through what appeared to be a translucent dome over the park, it seemed lit up with a dazzling array of sweeping spotlights. Chuck was certain he could hear music, joyous pumping music from a band or something. And for a moment he caught a glimpse of a turret from within the park that seemed as if it were part of a castle.

Wonder said nothing, instead silently allowing Chuck to take it all in. Finally he murmured, "It is impressive, isn't it?"

"From out here it looks like a prison," said Chuck.

Wonder made a rude, disdainful noise. "Nothing of the sort," he retorted. "A prison keeps evil in. We keep evil out. Mr. Jones, what you are seeing there is Wonderworld, the Safest Place in the World."

The limo turned suddenly, angling toward a wall, and Chuck watched, fascinated, as a huge metallic door slid aside. Chuck had not seen it before, and he suspected that he would not be able to locate it again. But here it was, big as life, and the limo sailed through into a darkened tunnel.

The limo seemed to go on forever through darkness, and then came to a large lighted area. People immediately approached the vehicle, pulling open the doors and helping the occupants out. One of them said briskly, "Heard there was a bit of a problem, Mr. Wonder."

"Nothing we couldn't handle—we being our splendid vehicles and this equally splendid chap here," and he patted Chuck on the shoulder.

The garage area was dim, but Chuck could tell from the way the voices echoed that they were in a vast parking bay. As his eyes slowly adjusted, he was able to make out visually what his ears had already told him. The place was like a football field, something that the former gym coach took to readily. Along a far wall were assorted vehicles of all shapes and sizes—limos, roadsters, runabouts—good God, a tank? A minitank? And . . . far off in the distant . . . was that some sort of air vehicle? Christ.

"You've got quite a setup here," Chuck said.

"Oh, you haven't seen the half of it," replied Wonder airily. "Come this way," and he gestured for Chuck to follow him. Chuck did so, Rommel padding after him. Even in this vast, intimidating place, Chuck took some measure of pride in the fact that everyone seemed interested in getting the hell out of Rommel's way.

Lunch, sounded in his head, and he was getting the distinct impression that he had pushed his dog's patience about as far as it was going to be pushed. "Rommel's hungry," he said. *Damned straight,* he heard.

"I'll make sure that we have something ready for him when we get down. Here we go," and he pointed toward a glistening elevator. The doors were sitting open, the inside a stunning display of grillwork. And interwoven into the grillwork was a metal representation of Moby Duck.

"He's your mascot, is he?" asked Chuck.

"Oh, he's the symbol of Wonderworld," said Wyatt. "The symbol of the entire Wonder Industry. He's the duck whose tail feathers you never yank." He raised a finger. "Or as we say around here . . . don't fuck with the duck."

"I'll remember that."

"Good." He did not sound as if he were kidding.

The four of them—Chuck, Rommel, Wyatt Wonder, and Connie—stepped into the elevator, the doors hissing shut behind them. The elevator started descending smoothly, possibly the smoothest ride on an elevator that Chuck had ever had.

And the longest. He glanced at his watch after long, silent seconds had passed, and he felt a gentle pressure building in his ears. Answering the unspoken question, Wonder said, "You are going to be descending a solid mile beneath the earth. Down into the place where the tour groups are never allowed—where not even most of the employees are allowed."

Chuck made a slow chewing motion to avoid his ears getting stopped up—with his sinuses bothering him, it was the last thing he needed. Rommel, apparently unperturbed by it, yawned widely. "Why so deep?" asked Chuck.

"Why, isn't it obvious, Chuck?" said Wonder. "To discourage attack by air. If our beloved president attempts to wipe me out with an air strike, all he'll wind up doing is destroying a beloved park—and thousands of innocent civilians, since the park is open twenty-four hours a day, and believe me, there's crowds here at all times."

"Why?"

"Because," said Wonder, as if stating the obvious, "where else would they want to be? I know of people who came to the park and stayed literally for days. We try to find people like that, of course, and escort them out. After all, people can get kind of surly when they're having fun for days on end. Ah, here we are."

The elevator was slowing down and finally halted, the doors hissing open. Wonder stepped out first, leading the way, followed by Connie. Rommel came right after her, and she put her hands on the sides of her short skirt as if afraid Rommel was going to make another probe.

Rommel glanced at Chuck. *What's her problem?*

"You know damned well," Chuck muttered.

Connie glanced from Rommel to Chuck, and there was something about her open, honest gaze that Chuck found refreshing, even pleasant. He smiled in return, feeling oddly self-conscious. They lagged several steps behind Wonder as he walked ahead of them, glancing and giving curt greetings to those employees who passed and greeted him.

"I don't think I caught your entire name," said Chuck softly.

"Consuela Lopez. Connie," she told him.

"Connie. That's a nice name."

She shrugged her small shoulders. "Serviceable," she said, sounding indifferent. "So, Mr. Jones . . ."

"Chuck."

"Chuck. You will enjoy working for Mr. Wonder."

Chuck half smiled at that. "I haven't exactly agreed to it yet."

"You'll find that Wyatt Wonder is a difficult man to refuse."

"I've refused some pretty difficult men," said Chuck. He was thinking of Quint, one of the heads of that mysterious outfit known as the Complex. Quint had wanted him to sign on as a psychic assassin. Chuck had not found that exactly an assignment to his liking and had refused, rather forcefully. He had been running ever since.

"No one quite like Wyatt Wonder," said Connie with certainty.

He looked at her thoughtfully. "Have you?"

She stopped in her tracks and stared at him, one sculpted eyebrow raised. "Have I what?"

"Refused him." Inside, Chuck couldn't believe he was asking the question. But there was something about her that pushed and prodded him, that provoked him. And prompted him to provoke her in return.

"That," she said, "is none of your business." There was no heat in her response, merely a statement of fact.

"You're right," he said evenly. He slowed his pace as she

sped hers up, and looked down at Rommel. *Smooth,* Rommel informed him.

"Thanks," Chuck replied sourly.

Instead of thinking about how he had stumbled over his own intentions, Chuck concentrated on studying his surroundings. There were framed posters lining the hallways, promoting various movies that Wonder Films had produced over the years. Chuck had seen a good number of them, and indeed still felt a bit in awe of where he was.

Wonderworld was legendary, after all. He had never been there before, never been this far west, really. Not with all the predictions of the Big One sending quakes through the ground that would sink the entire state once and for all. It was a fear that he had never quite gotten over, although they had proven secondary to his ceaseless wanderings and quest for peace.

He passed small models in cases that were obviously used for animator reference for various Wonder characters. There was Moby Duck, there was Pistol Pete, Dapper Dan the Pelican, dozens more. He felt as if he were reliving his childhood. His friends smiled out at him from their glass enclosures, and he was certain that here was a wink, or there a slight nod of the head as if to say, "Hey, Chuck, we're alive. We're here. As soon as the lights go out we'll leap right out of these crummy cases and have the same good times we always did."

Back when it was possible to have good times. Back when he didn't care that the sky was always gray, or that adults went around with a slightly haunted look on their faces, and one eye cast perpetually over their shoulder.

Ahead of him, Connie opened a door and gestured. Chuck started toward it but Rommel hurtled past him as if shot from a cannon. Chuck knew immediately what was going on, even if his nose didn't share Rommel's sensitivity. By the time he got to the room and peered in, Rommel had already chowed down on two raw steaks and was beginning his third. What prompted Chuck's eyes to widen in surprise was that the room was piled high with meat, enough to satisfy a hundred Rommels (well, maybe a dozen

Rommels; there probably wasn't enough meat in North America to satisfy a hundred of those car-sized, carnivorous monsters).

"Your boss works quickly," observed Chuck.

"My boss is accustomed to being prepared for any eventuality," replied Connie quietly. "This way."

Chuck glanced over his shoulder and said to Rommel, "You going to be all right here?"

Rommel didn't even look at him but shot back a quick thought. *You're kidding, right?*

"Right. I'm kidding. Pardon me for asking." Chuck fought down a smile and did not succeed.

He turned and followed Connie, who seemed to be studying him with new curiosity. "What, you and that dog talk to each other?"

"Sure," said Chuck airily. "We share a psychic rapport, augmented by the fact that I'm one of the most powerful telekinetics in the country, if not the planet."

She smiled thinly. "Ask a silly question."

He nodded. He'd been through this before, and by this point was usually giving the same answer every time—and getting pretty much the same type of response.

"In here," and she gestured to another room. The doors were large and metal, and they hissed open, to reveal—nothing. Just blackness, so thick that he knew if he stepped in there his hand would be invisible in front of his face.

Were they trying to make him a prisoner? Well, hell, he was a mile below surface, with concrete and steel—or whatever metal that was—above him. He was, to all intents and purposes, a prisoner now. How much more could they possibly do to him?

"In for a penny," he muttered, and walked in.

The door slid shut with an overpowering *clang* and he stood in darkness. Sure enough, he couldn't see a damn thing.

He stood there for long moments, calm and at peace. If they thought a little darkness was going to seriously throw him, they were going to be badly disappointed. Chuck was far too at peace, far too evenly balanced, to be jolted by

something as trivial as an absence of light. And the
silence—total. Absolute silence, so complete that it seemed
to have its own life. *The silence was deafening.* How
clichéd, and how frequently he'd read the phrase in cheap
novels. But for all the times he'd read it, it had never had
any real meaning to it. That was the problem with clichés.
They become so comfortingly familiar that they lose any
sense of importance.

But dammit, the silence was deafening. What made it
deafening was that, in the effort to hear *something,* for
pity's sake, you become overwhelmed by the sound of your
breathing, of your heart pounding in your chest and your
pulse in your temple. And every time your eyelid closes, it
sounds like someone yanking down a windowshade. Your
sweat starts to drip out of your pores, each drop falling
plink, plink to the ground, crashing like a cascade of water,
and pretty soon you want to just shut down your entire body
because of the noise from everywhere in it, just everywhere, filling your ears and your mind with deafening
silence.

Some damned cliché that was.

Within five minutes the calm, balanced Chuck Simon
was starting to get edgy. He wiped away the sweat beading
on his forehead, which was odd in and of itself considering
how cool it was in the place. So he spoke, jumping ever so
slightly at his own voice and pleased that no one could see it.

"Wonder!" (Jump.) "I don't know what your game is,
but I don't intend to play along with it. Come out. Put the
lights on, and tell me what's going on, or I'm leaving. And
I have a sneaking suspicion that we both know that if I want
to leave, there's no way in heaven or hell that you're going
to be able to stop me."

There was silence for either a second more or an
eternity—hard to tell—and then suddenly . . .

THE LIGHT.

It overwhelmed Chuck, as if it were a thing alive, hitting
him with such force from all sides that he staggered. In his
ears, in his mind, accompanying the light, was music. It
steamrolled over him, crashing onto him like waves in the

surf, throwing him completely off kilter. It echoed and reechoed, a bizarre cacophony that was part angelic choir, part hallelujah chorus, as played by a heavy metal band with a reggae beat. Such a staggering agglomeration, and yet somehow it seemed to all blend together somehow. Light and images came to his mind unbidden, exploding behind his eyeballs, dazzling color pinwheeling and sparking off in all directions.

And the voice. God in heaven, THE VOICE, and it intoned, sepulchral and doom-sounding. *"IN THE BEGINNING—WERE THE PRODUCTION COMPANIES."*

The walls around him sprang to life, and he was completely surrounded by images flashing by at dazzling speed. Here and there he managed to separate a picture from the montage, moving at blinding velocities, the sum total making an impact and yet making it almost impossible to pull out a distinguishing visual.

Dozens of movie logos, hundreds of stars and starlets, has-beens and never-wases, hurtled past.

"DOZENS OF PRODUCTION COMPANIES, HUNDREDS OF INDIES. IN TV, THERE WERE 300 CABLE CHANNELS. THERE WAS CONFUSION, GREED. DECISIONS WERE MADE WITHOUT SENSE, WITHOUT INTELLIGENCE WITHOUT—A PLAN."

"A plan?" gasped out Chuck, sinking to his knees. He wanted to get the hell out of there, tried to bring his TK to bear so that he could force open the door, but his mind was too scrambled. Colors were running riot past him, images were a total mishmash. He was trying to decipher them instead of take them as a totality, and that was a mistake. For instance, he wasn't sure, but he thought he'd just seen a very young Ronald Reagan click his ruby slippers together and say something about washing that man right out of his hair. And Reagan was machine gunning Asians while he was doing it.

"YES . . . A PLAN. I'LL TELL YOU ABOUT IT . . ."

Rommel dropped his fifth steak, his jaw going slack. He staggered, barraged. Through his link with Chuck he saw images (black and white, of course) coming fast and furious, and it was too much for the dog's far-less-complex mind to cope with. As a matter of self-protection, Rommel's mind quite simply shut down, and the massive German shepherd keeled over.

"A PLAN—A PLAN THAT WAS CONCEIVED IN THE MIND OF: WYATT WONDER."

From a hundred different directions, Wyatt Wonder's face appeared.

"YEARS, DECADES EARLIER," the proud voice boasted—and Chuck felt his inner ear shaking—*"WYATT'S FATHER, WES WONDER, FOUNDED THE WONDER FILMS COMPANY, BUILT THE FIRST WONDERWORLD PARK. MOVIES AND ENTERTAINMENT CONCEIVED OF FOR ENTIRE FAMILIES TO SHARE. BUT AS THIS GREAT COUNTRY OF OURS FELL APART, AS NUCLEAR FAMILIES MELTED DOWN, SO TOO DID WONDER FILMS, UNTIL IT TEETERED ON THE EDGE OF BANKRUPTCY. THE FIRM WAS AN INDUSTRY JOKE.*

"BUT WYATT WONDER, THE SON OF WES WONDER, STOPPED THE LAUGHTER. HE DEVELOPED A LINE OF FILMS FOR ALL AGES. AND HIS GREATEST MASTERSTROKE—HE TRANSFORMED WONDERWORLD INTO WHAT PEOPLE REALLY NEEDED IN THESE TIMES: A PLACE OF SAFETY, WHERE PEOPLE CAN RELAX AND KNOW THAT THE AIR THEY BREATHE IS CLEAN, THE WATER PURE, THE THOUGHTS UNGOVERNED."

From all around Chuck were more and more pictures, faster and faster. Here there were cities literally crumbling, and yet there were images of a smiling Wyatt, of happy children running and laughing as off to the side others felt their skin mottling and rotting away from acid rain. And here were children hanging in trees dotting the sides of Wonderworld's Main Street, in stark contrast to leveled rain forests where the only sign of life were the corpses of small animals littering the landscape.

"WONDER FILMS GREW AND GREW. MERGER

LAWS HAD BEEN RELAXED TO GIVE SECRETLY GOVERNMENT-BACKED INDUSTRIES THE CHANCE TO GRAB UP AS MUCH AS POSSIBLE WITHOUT INTERFERENCE. BUT WYATT WONDER TURNED THAT TO HIS ADVANTAGE, BUYING OUT ONE MOVIE STUDIO AFTER ANOTHER. 'DUCK AMOK' SCREAMED THE SAME TRADE PAPERS THAT HAD ONCE PREDICTED WONDER'S DEMISE. IT TOOK FAR LESS TIME THAN ANYONE HAD EXPECTED, BECAUSE WYATT WONDER HAD THE DRIVE, THE VISION, THE PLAN.

"WYATT SAW ALL THAT THERE WAS, AND MADE IT GOOD. EVENTUALLY, WONDER CONTROLLED THE ENTIRE ENTERTAINMENT INDUSTRY. IF IT WAS MADE, WONDER FILMS MADE IT. IF WONDER FILMS DIDN'T WANT IT MADE, IT DIDN'T GET MADE. AND NOBODY MINDED, BECAUSE WONDER FILMS WERE QUALITY. WONDER FILMS CARED. WYATT WONDER CARES, ABOUT YOU, ABOUT ME. ABOUT THE LITTLE GUY."

Chuck tried to find his calm center, to reestablish balance, but it was utterly hopeless. The sound, the flashing lights, the barrage of sensation that had followed the period of lack of sensation, had caught him flatfooted and he had not even come close to recovering.

"YOU SEE . . . THE GOVERNMENT CONTROLS THE PEOPLE'S MINDS . . . BUT WYATT WONDER CONTROLS THEIR HEARTS. AND WYATT WONDER, THE GREATEST SUCCESS STORY IN AMERICAN HISTORY—WYATT WONDER, THE HEART AND SOUL OF AMERICAN ENTERTAINMENT—WANTS YOU!"

And finally, Chuck let the cooling wave of unconsciousness mercifully slip over him, and he passed out.

4

IT HAD BEEN the middle of the night, Eastern Standard Time, when Wyatt Wonder had phoned The Man. Which meant, of course, that Wyatt had awakened him, since the president was notorious for believing the adage about early to bed.

That Wyatt had been able to get in touch with the president at all was amazing, for virtually no one outside of the president's cabinet was capable of accomplishing that feat. The president had a private line to the phone next to his bed. The phone number for it was chosen at random by a computer and changed every three weeks. And yet somehow Wyatt Wonder always managed to have the number at his fingertips, and he would call with impunity when the mood struck him. The president had yet to figure out how the man did it and, chances were, never would.

The point, however, was this—the president had been roused. Once roused, he could not go back to sleep, even if he had been so inclined. And the rage that was building in him definitely disinclined him.

He sat there in bed for long moments, squeezing the phone until his knuckles turned white and his fingers went numb. Next to him his wife slept dreamless dreams, her customary combination of alcohol and knockout drops sending her into the sort of slumber that her desire to escape from the bleak hideousness of her life required. The intensity of her wish to escape from the man she was wedded to was evident only in the relish with which she welcomed the sleep hours. A year in the future, she would deliberately overdose on her knockout drops and slip away during the night, once and for all. At the time she would do it, she would be certain that her husband wouldn't care. She would be correct.

But that was a year away, and for now she dreamt of nothing while the man next to her fantasized various and sundry forms of death and torture for the man who ruled the entertainment industry of America, Wyatt Wonder. Wonder and his aged, senile father.

Not releasing his grip on the phone in the slightest, he barked a four-syllable name into it. The phone, like Wonder's, was equipped with the latest name-responsive pre-encodement. It lacked the whimsy of Wonder's, although the president was already in such a foul mood that knowing the nickname he had been given in the Wonder scheme-of-things could scarely have blackened it much more.

Mere moments after his name had been spat out, like expectoration, into the phone, Terwilliger answered the ring. Unlike the president, he had not been asleep. Rumor had it that he never did. The story going around was that Terwilliger had reduced his eight hours' sleep each night to seven, then six, and so on by degrees over a period of months until he had reduced it to one and then none. It wasn't true, of course. But it very nearly could have been.

"Yes, sir," for Terwilliger knew with certainty who it was. For that matter he knew what he was calling about, for Terwilliger's sources were the best and he'd known the moment the hit had failed.

"I understand," said The Man slowly, carefully, trying to control his fury with about as much success as one would have stifling a volcano by means of dropping a large cork in the top, "I understand that Mr. Wyatt Wonder met with a *near* accident."

"Yes, sir." Terwilliger's voice was carefully neutral. Not a question, not a statement of surprise, he told himself. Don't give away what you do know or don't know. Two reasons for that: First, you don't want the president thinking that you were holding back information from him or, contrariwise, thinking that you weren't on top of things enough to already know what was going on. You dwell in the gray area of should-have-known-and-probably-did. That's first.

Second is that the line was not tapped, couldn't possibly in any way be tapped, except you always assume that it is. Always.

Always.

"A near accident," said Terwilliger from the grayness.

"Near." The repetition from The Man was in order to put not too fine a point on it. "Do you have any idea why someone would *try* and kill Mr. Wonder?"

And fail. Those were the unspoken words at the end of the sentence, the words that made all the difference. Terwilliger knew this, knew what the question really was. Namely: You moron. What the hell happened? I order a simple plucking of a long-persistent thorn and you can't even handle that, you miserable clod?!

Terwilliger answered the question by not answering it. "Mr. Wonder has many enemies, sir. He—and America, of course—can consider it lucky that something very unexpected must have occurred in order to stave off the attack."

The president was silent for a moment. "Unexpected."

"Very," affirmed Terwilliger.

It was like playing a chess game, for the president knew the unspoken rules too. For a moment Terwilliger thought that the president was going to order him to come to the office for an emergency meeting, but instead he spoke even more slowly, his mind clearly running ahead of himself. "Unexpected in the way of a one-time occurrence, unlikely ever to be a factor again. Because if so," added the president, sounding excessively concerned, "Mr. Wonder is really going to have to watch himself."

"It's difficult to ascertain from the facts as presented,"

said Terwilliger. "But I'm sure we'll know more in the morning."

"See that we do," said The Man sharply, and broke the connection. He never said good-bye. He didn't have to.

By nine A.M. the next morning, Terwilliger was in the president's office. Terwilliger could tell that the president had not slept well, if at all. His normally sharp gaze was simply nasty and fierce, and he spoke with a staccato meter rather than the careful and reasoned one he usually used.

"Let's cut through the shit," he said before Terwilliger had even fully sat down. "You want to tell me what the story is, Terwilliger? This awful event that occurred—we must know the full facts—if we are to make sure that nothing like this happens again."

You mean so that we don't fuck up again, Terwilliger silently said mirthlessly. He considered a moment, composing his thoughts. When he spoke it was in the same no-nonsense briefing voice that he would have used if addressing the joint chiefs. "I've been compiling reports from the various agents who just happened to be on the scene and survived. Also, there were a couple of street people who were watching from hiding, plus proprietors of stores—a grocery store and a comic-book store were completely destroyed."

"Compensate the owners," said the president briskly. "Although frankly I won't miss the comic store. Comics are perverted instruments of sick creative minds, if you ask me. If Wonder didn't own the comic-book companies . . ." His voice trailed off a moment as he had accidentally reminded himself of that which so irritated him.

"They have all been debriefed," said Terwilliger briskly. "Their descriptions, along with our agents, have been broken down into bytes and we have a computer re-creation of the event loaded in."

"You've had a busy night," said the president. For just the briefest of moments the president actually sounded— God help him, thought Terwilliger—appreciative.

"Comes with the job," replied Terwilliger. "Lights, please."

The lights of the Oval Office automatically dimmed, and on the far wall a portion slid back to reveal an enlarged computer screen.

A moment later computer-animated figures appeared on the screen, lifelike and perfectly symmetrical. It was an exact re-creation of the scene that had been played out in real life only the previous night.

"Sky view," said Terwilliger briskly. The computer promptly angled upward, giving the sky-high viewpoint of the event that was about to happen, frozen in waiting for Terwilliger's order. "Play out at one-half speed," he said.

As the failed assassination began, Terwilliger narrated it, tapping key moments on the screen with his long finger and speaking in a calm, unhurried manner. "Here is Wonder's car coming around the corner, preceded by his escort vehicle. As you can see, the setup was initially perfect. Street-level view, please," and the computer obediently brought the angle down so that it was as if the president were sitting right at curbside. Ring-side seat for the big show.

"South side view," Terwilliger added, and the picture swung around so that the fake old man could be seen bringing his weapon around in slow motion. "See that the lead vehicle was taken out by this individual here. West side view. Now there"—and he pointed—"is a garbage truck coming in, blocking the means of escape. A fire is starting here."

"What are those streaks entering the picture from over-head?"

"Unknown assailants from the upper floor of a building on the north side," said Terwilliger quietly.

"Unknown."

"And unmourned, because apparently they failed in their mission and paid with their lives as you will see."

The re-creation played itself out and suddenly the president sat forward, frowning. Terwilliger was already anticipating it and said, "Freeze frame."

"Who the hell is that?" said the president.

There was a man who had seemed to come out of nowhere, and he was hanging on to the side of the garbage truck, apparently struggling with the driver.

"That, sir, is the unexpected. The unanticipated. The x-factor. Magnify view of point three-zero-five"

The screen rearranged itself and was filled with a face.

"Some guy with a moustache looks like," said the president. The face was undetailed—there had been conflicting reports of hair color, clothing, and the like. Two eyes, nose, mouth, relatively short hair it looked like, some sort of moustache. "He looks like any one of millions of guys. You got a line on him?"

"No, sir," said Terwilliger. "Not yet. But here's something interesting. Point of view from point three-zero-five."

The computer rearranged the picture, and what it presented was a postulation of what the mystery man was seeing from the point where he was at that moment. The president was seeing it too—the top of the building, burning, frying men who had moments before tried to kill the king of cartoons.

"Rewind view using projected path of current point of view."

Time ran backward as the side of the garbage truck receded, and the building top put itself back together again. There were the men, hanging out the windows, firing down upon Wyatt Wonder, brought back to pretend life through the miracle of computer graphics.

"Forward, one-quarter speed," said Terwilliger.

Even more slowly now the events unfolded themselves once more. There went the explosion, there went the men, but . . .

"Why?" said the President, annoyed with himself. He knew there was something here he was missing and he didn't know what. "Why did the men up there blow up? Why are you showing me this?"

"Remember, sir," said Terwilliger, "you're seeing this from the point of view of our mystery man, as near as we can determine. The comic-shop owner swears that the x-factor man was watching the upper stories at all times. That means he was watching when it blew up. That means—"

"What?" said the president impatiently.

"I don't know," admitted Terwilliger. "It means to me, somehow, that this man knew it was going to blow. The cause that we have been able to determine is a misfiring launcher. But he couldn't have known it was going to misfire. There's something about this man that doesn't fall into place, and I don't like it at all."

"I'm glad you don't like it," said the president tartly. "It's not as if I'm exactly ecstatic with the turn of events, you know. Run the damned thing forward from a normal angle."

Terwilliger did so, and the president chewed his lip as he watched Wonder slip through the trap, although he did take some measure of satisfaction seeing his nemesis stow away in a garbage truck. "But, now, wait," he said confused. "Run it back. There. That thing there. How in the hell did a horse get involved in all this? You see there? There's a horse running across the street, climbing into the cab of the—" His voice caught. "Shit. What the hell is that?"

"It's not a horse," said Terwilliger definitely. "People were very confused at that point, with all the smoke and hysteria. Our best guess is that it's a bear."

"The guy works with a bear?! Who the hell *is* he? Paul Bunyan?"

"Paul Bunyan worked with an ox, sir."

"I don't care if he worked with a goddamn singing crab!" snapped the president. "I want this goddam x-factor unknown person and his bear! You read me? I want to know what's going on, and dammit, I'm going to. And you're going to tell me, or it's your ass. Got that?"

"Yes, sir," said Terwilliger, who definitely had it.

5

SLOWLY CHUCK BECAME aware of the soft pillow beneath his head. He became equally aware that it had been ages since he had really felt remotely comfortable. Mostly when he had been sleeping in recent months, it had been with one part of his mind always at the ready, always trying to be sensitive to imminent danger. And it had been catch-as-catch-can, sleeping in the backs of cars or under trees or curled up in ditches somewhere, or in a strange, uncomfortable bed in a strange, uncomfortable town. He had not been relaxed in ages.

He half turned and ran his fingers over the smoothness of the sheets beneath him. They felt crisp and freshly laundered. His eyes still closed, he scratched at his chest and noticed in a distant way that it was bare.

There was silence all around him. Wherever he was, it was peaceful and secluded and very, very quiet. Perhaps he was dreaming. Perhaps he was dead. Perhaps he would never know if he didn't open his eyes. Then it would never be ruined. But on the other hand, his questions would never be answered.

He imagined tossing a coin and it came up heads.

Slowly he opened his eyes.

Eyes were staring back at him.

Chuck's eyes widened from narrow slits to full wakefulness. There was a man staring at him, an old man. His hair was white and thinning, but his face—it was round, cherubic. Chuck could easily imagine what this man looked like as a child, because much of that child was still reflected in the face that regarded him now. The eyes that were studying Chuck were as blue as Chuck's own, and they had a mixture of secretiveness and knowledge in them.

"I can walk," whispered the old man.

Slowly Chuck propped himself up on one elbow. He could see now that the man was seated in some sort of mobile chair. There were a few inches between the bottom of the chair and the ground. The chair was just hovering there, on a several inches-high cushion of air. Or maybe magnetism, like the cross-country, super-expensive bullet train that had been instituted from San Francisco to New York.

"You can walk," Chuck said, not fully comprehending.

"Oh, yes. Yes indeed." The old man gave a conspiratorial look. "But don't tell anyone. You're the first person I've told. Swear, on your honor."

Now this was a serious matter to Chuck, and he would not make such a promise lightly. But the old man seemed so determined, and besides, the old man was clearly not all there anyway. He probably couldn't walk, and even if he could, of what interest was it to Chuck, really. "I swear," said Chuck. "But why did you tell me?"

"Because you look interesting," said the old man.

Chuck tilted his head and studied the old man. "You seem familiar somehow. Who—?"

"*Mr. Wonder!*"

Chuck looked up in surprise. Connie was standing in the doorway, hands on her hips, an annoyed expression on her face. She wore a powder-blue dress, cut inward at the midsection on either side and revealing crescent-shaped expanses of her flat, tanned belly. She shook her head. "You know you're not supposed to be away from your suite. Everyone is very upset. How did you get away?"

Now Chuck was nodding slowly. "That's it. You're Wes Wonder. Wyatt's father. My God, I used to watch you when I was very little. When you'd host the hour-long TV show, *The Colorful World of Wonder*."

"Why of course," said Wes. "But what do you mean 'used to'?" There was confusion on that round face. "Don't you still?"

Chuck blinked in surprise, uncertain of what to say. He looked up at Connie for guidance, and the woman quickly said, "Now, Mr. Wonder, that's enough. You really have to be going now."

Wonder held up a scolding finger and smiled in an avuncular fashion. "Now, young lady—no 'Mr. Wonder' here. I'm Uncle Wes to all my little friends."

"Of course, Uncle Wes," said Connie gamely, and behind her a couple of uniformed security guards, with small representations of the Wonderworld castle stitched on their coveralls, had appeared. "Now these nice men will bring you back to your suite."

Wonder turned and looked back at Chuck, smiling. He held out a hand, which Chuck shook firmly. There was a surprising amount of strength in the old man's grip. "I shall be talking to you, young man," he said. "And I expect you to watch the program. I have a busy schedule, but I always make time to host the program. Not many executives would do something like that."

"No, sir."

Wonder dropped his voice to a near whisper. "Not a word of our discussion, remember."

"Count on me, sir."

Wonder worked a small joystick on his armrest, and the chair obediently swiveled around and glided noiselessly out the door, between the two guards. The door shut behind him, with Connie stepping lightly in just before the doors closed.

They stood there a moment, regarding each other. Chuck sat up in bed, blanket covering him. He was wearing flannel pajama pants, he realized, which was interesting considering he'd never worn any such things in his life. Made his legs itch.

"That was Wes Wonder," said Chuck, as if doing a reality check.

She nodded, leaning against the door frame, her arms folded. "It most certainly was."

"Wyatt's father. The founder of the entire Wonder industry."

"Founder," she agreed. "But it was going to pot under his regime when he refused to change with the times. Wyatt saved it and made it the thriving enterprise it—"

Chuck waved it off, swinging his feet down to the metal ground. "You can save the promotional announcements. I had a bellyful of them earlier." He paused. *The Colorful World of Wonder* hasn't been on the air for two decades."

"You know that. I know that." She inclined her head in the direction that Wes Wonder had been taken and shrugged, her expression saying it all.

"But he doesn't." He paused, considering that. "Where's Rommel?"

"He's fine."

"I want him here immediately. And then we're leaving."

"That would be unwise."

He frowned at that. "Are you saying," he asked slowly, "that you will refuse to let me leave?"

"No, I'm saying that that's a good way to get killed. You helped thwart an assassination attempt by the U.S. Government, and wipe that look off your face. If you don't think they're capable of that, you haven't been living in this country for the early part of this century."

"Oh, I'm aware of that," said Chuck. "It's just that—"

"That you realize they'll be gunning for you." She nodded and walked over toward him and then sat on a chair that was next to the head of the bed. "They'll be watching the area like hawks. They'll be looking for you. It would be wise for you to stay put until things settle down . . . unless you enjoy the thought of being hunted by the government."

Why should today be different? he thought.

He stared at her and frowned. She was so calm. Chuck, with his psychic sensitivity, was always picking up free-floating sensations from people. Not specific thoughts so much as general impulses, feelings, and attitudes. Thoughts of aggressiveness came through particularly strongly.

From Connie, though, he picked up little. She was very much someone at peace, calm—like himself. Someone who must search for and find that inner area, that internal core, of neutrality. Perhaps even more effectively than did he.

"I want Rommel," he said again.

"Later."

"Now."

She nodded once and stood. "Follow me," she said.

"You mind if I get dressed?"

"Oh. Of course." She stood and walked briskly out of the room, saying, "Your clothes are in that closet over there."

He went to the closet and opened it. There were clothes in there, all right. Nothing that he'd ever seen before, a very impressive array, and all—he checked quickly—in his size.

This was getting to be very, very interesting.

They walked down the hallway together, Chuck now wore black pants and black shirt, with black sneakers. Connie was looking him up and down and shaking her head. "Not very California," she observed, "unless you're planning on breaking into someone's house."

"I look good in black," he said.

"You look like Errol Flynn."

"Who?"

She shrugged. "Forget it. Over here."

She indicated a room and Chuck already sensed that Rommel was inside. And he also sensed . . . well, he wasn't sure what he sensed.

The door slid open and Chuck stopped in the doorway, a grin of disbelief splitting his face.

It appeared that Rommel had died and gone to doggie heaven. The room seemed to have been set up specifically to accommodate him. There was food—large steaks, raw and dripping, and biscuits—at spots all over the room.

There was a large, soft cushion in the middle of the room that Rommel lay on, his head on his paws, and he was watching a holo vid program rerun of some movie with a dog in it. At a far edge of the room was a fire hydrant with drainage grating surrounding it and, right nearby, a chute, both to accommodate the obvious. There was an amazing assortment of doggie toys, ranging from the innocuous to an oversize hard-rubber leg dangling from the ceiling like a punching bag, the leg clothed in the uniform blue of a mailman. That item, in particular, already had significant teeth marks on it.

"Rommel!" said Chuck in amazement.

Rommel didn't even glance at him. *Yeah?*

"What do you think you're doing?"

Watching vid. You have a problem with that?

"Since when do you care about that?" Chuck took a step into the room, looking around in amazement. He leaned on an exercise treadmill. "All you care about is food, defecating, killing, and humping."

My belly's full for the first time in ages, I just defecated five minutes ago, nothing's attacking me, and . . . He paused and looked at Chuck. *You got someone for me to hump?*

"Not handy, no. Don't you want to get out of here? Get on the road? Get back to—"

Hunger? Running? Picking rocks out of my paws and branches out of my fur? That sounds like loads of fun.

"But we're prisoners here!"

"No you're not," Connie said quickly, apparently choosing not to question the nature of the one-sided conversation. "Leave anytime."

"Not without Rommel," said Chuck. "Come on, Rommel. Now."

Rommel didn't move.

"NOW!"

Slowly Rommel turned his massive head toward Chuck, and there was fury in his eyes.

Connie automatically took a step back, for an angry Rommel was a sight to make one's blood stop. She tugged on Chuck's arm and said urgently, "Come on. Come on, I don't like this."

But Chuck pulled away from her and strode toward Rommel, stopping right in front of the dog, blocking the view of the vid, his hands on his hips, firmness in his face. Rommel faced him, his tail straight out, teeth bared, a low growling in his throat.

"Rommel," said Chuck in a slow, measured tone, "we're leaving. Now."

No.

"Then I'm leaving without you."

Fine.

"Is that what you want? Because if it is, fine. It may not be a free country anymore," said Chuck harshly, "but as far as I'm concerned you're free to do what you want. You want Wyatt Wonder to be your new master and provider, fine. He obviously can do a better job than I can." Hurt and rage bubbled up in him and he tried to brush it aside, to stay calm and balanced. He was only partly successful. "Then this is it, Rommel. This is good-bye."

Rommel stared at him. *You're not leaving.*

"Oh, yes I am. This whole thing smacks too much of the Complex. I'm not hanging around to make the same mistake. Are you coming with me?"

This time Rommel said nothing, although the growling had stopped.

Chuck stood there a brief time longer, waiting for some response. None was forthcoming, and he turned and stalked toward the door, fists clenched, seething.

Please?

He stopped and turned, and his jaw dropped in surprise.

He'd never seen Rommel do anything like it before. The huge dog was up on his hind legs, forelegs brought up and just under his muzzle. And in his eyes—genuine pleading. And Chuck thought, *My God, he's begging.*

Please? Rommel said again.

Rommel had never asked anything of him before, ever, aside from food. And even that had never been so much asking as preemptory demands in a somewhat high-handed tone. Sometimes even with a trace of impatience, as if Rommel couldn't understand why fate had paired him with this slow-to-respond human.

Chuck slowly walked toward Rommel and stopped in front of him. Rommel didn't move from the begging position, something that Chuck was unaware that Rommel even knew. Theirs was not the sort of relationship where Chuck ran Rommel through clever doggie tricks and rewarded him with a biscuit for catching a Frisbee in his teeth or some such nonsense.

"This means a lot to you," said Chuck in surprise.

I just want some time off from running, said Rommel. *I'll probably get bored here eventually and we can go back to being cold and uncomfortable and paranoid. The good life. But just for now—?*

Chuck scratched him back of his ears. "All right," he said softly. "All right, Rommel. For a little while."

Good. Rommel dropped down to the ground, putting his head back on his forepaws. *Now get out of the way, you're blocking the screen.*

"Sure."

Chuck turned and walked away, leaving Rommel in the lap of luxury. He walked past Connie without a word and into the hallway, and she followed him. Chuck turned toward her the moment the doors hissed shut. "It appears we're staying awhile."

"That's good to hear."

It had not been Connie who responded. Instead Chuck turned to find himself staring at Wyatt Wonder, who had an inordinately pleased smile on his face.

"I don't appreciate your splitting my animal's loyalties," said Chuck tersely. "And I don't appreciate being barraged with a multi-media presentation so overwhelming that I passed out."

"It wasn't just my little presentation, Mr. Simon," replied Wonder. "Our doctors checked you over. Were you suffering from sinus headaches? It was more than that. You had some sort of residual infection in your bloodstream—at least that's what my med corp discovered after you passed out and they ran some blood tests on you. Seems to be pollution connected. You been swimming anytime recently in a place you shouldn't have been, or breathing in air in a particularly polluted area?"

Chuck knew damned well he had. Not too long ago, in the polluted waters in Colorado, in a stream that a factory had been using to dump God-only-knew-what chemicals. It had made him damned sick, and something in his constitution had enabled him to shake it in record time. Or at least he thought he had. Obviously he hadn't been one hundred percent successful.

Upon getting no response, Wonder continued, "My meds shot you up with antibiotics. Your head should be clear about now, and you can take comfort that your bloodstream is clear too, Mr. Simon."

Chuck nodded and then stopped.

"Oh, yes," said Wonder, upon noting Chuck's expression. "I know your name. My med corps also did a retina scan and I ran it through my computers, which are privy to some fascinating information. Chuck Simon, code named Psi-Man. You're quite a remarkable gentleman. It certainly explains how you were able to save my life. That was probably just routine for you."

Connie was looking from one to the other of them in confusion. "I don't understand," she said.

"Oh, it's quite simple really, Connie. According to what my computer ties have turned up—all top secret, you know—Mr. Simon here is a very formidable telekinetic. He also has a psychic link with that amazingly huge canine of his. It appears, however, that Mr. Simon is on the run. Apparently he was an employee of the Complex, our government's espionage and internal affairs arm, and departed under somewhat violent circumstances. Would you care to elaborate, Mr. Simon?"

Chuck looked at him stoically, and Connie said, "The Complex? They really exist?"

"Oh, they do indeed," said Wonder very cheerfully. "And they wanted Mr. Simon here to be an assassin. Isn't that right?"

"I don't appreciate your invasion of my privacy," Chuck said.

As if Chuck hadn't spoken, Wonder said, "He seemed perfect for them. Not only is his mind powerful, but he is a master of aikido, a marvelous system of hand-to-hand defense. But Mr. Simon also is a rather peaceful soul—a member of the Society of Friends, or Quakers, to be specific, and becoming an assassin seemed against his grain. Have I got all this correct, Mr. Simon? To sum up, Connie, what we have here is a fugitive telekinetic aikido-master Quaker and his telepathic German shepherd. Mr. Simon, welcome to the land of movies. Your life is what we in the industry refer to as 'High Concept.'"

"Thank you," said Chuck dryly. He glanced at Connie to see what sort of impact all this had on the young Mexican woman, and surprisingly she seemed quite calm about it all. Considering where she worked and who she worked for, this might indeed qualify as nothing more than business as usual.

"Miss Lopez, you may consider making Mr. Simon comfortable your top priority. Your normal secretarial duties can be handled by others. Mr. Simon—Chuck"—and his voice dropped to a more serious tone from his annoyingly bantering one— "I appreciate your irritation over my invading your privacy, and for that I do apologize. But I did not get to where I am today by being ignorant. You used your considerable talents to save my life, and for that you have my undying gratitude. I think if you worked for me, as a bodyguard and right-hand man, we would both be quite well off. You would have security, and I would know that I have a man of honor guarding my back. You must, however, follow your own inner voices. Stay as long as you wish, and of course go wherever you wish, aside from those areas marked 'off limits.' Connie, why don't you bring Chuck to the surface and show him the park."

"Yes, sir."

Wonder turned and started to walk away, and Chuck abruptly said, "Haven."

Wonder stopped and looked back at him. "I beg your pardon?"

"Haven." Chuck took a step forward. "Does that mean anything to you?"

"Aside from the obvious dictionary definition, no. Should it?"

"I'm not sure," said Chuck. "If it did . . . would you tell me?"

Wonder paused a moment. "Of course. If it suited my purposes." And then he turned and walked away, noiselessly on the carpeted hallway.

6

TERWILLIGER LOOKED UP from his desk as his aide stuck his head in the door and said, "He's here, sir."

Terwilliger's office was sparse and dark, much like the man himself. His desk was compulsively clean, with not so much as a speck of dust in evidence. As a result, the opened door sent in a sliver of light that in most offices would have gone unnoticed, but here was like a star exploding. Terwilliger inclined his head slightly and the aide withdrew. Moments later the door opened wider and a man entered.

He seemed almost ethereal in nature, as if he were not really there. Despite the darkness of the room, he wore sunglasses that were cobalt blue. He was holding a hat and coat in his arms, and his hair was close-cropped and gray. He tilted his head, the only hint that Terwilliger had that the man was looking at him. "Terwilliger," he said.

"Sit down, Quint," said Terwilliger, gesturing to the chair directly in front of his desk.

Quint sat noiselessly, which may not seem particularly interesting. But when people sit, there's always some sort of noise. A chair squeaking, or the sound of air exhaling from cushions . . . something. The man named Quint made no sound at all. If Terwilliger hadn't been looking straight at him, he might not even have realized that Quint was in the room.

Quint made him nervous, and there were not many people in the world about whom Terwilliger would say that.

"It's good to see you, Quint," he said conversationally.

"It's necessary to see me." Quint spoke barely above a whisper, as if every aspect of him was in total control. "There is something on your mind, and you feel I can help you."

"How's the Complex going?" asked Terwilliger.

"Please get to the point."

"How's the Complex going?" he repeated, making it clear that he was going to take his time.

"Fine," said Quint evenly.

"Heard you had a bit of a set-to a few months back."

"Nothing we couldn't handle."

Terwilliger steepled his fingers and leaned forward. "Eighty-six the glasses, Quint. I want to see your face."

Quint didn't move. "I don't see that as being necessary." The quiet voice had a slight tint of menace to it.

But the implied threat bothered Terwilliger not at all. "You answer to the Council, Quint, and the Council answers to me. And, goddammit, you will remember who's in charge. Now take the glasses off."

Quint sat there a moment longer and then slowly reached up and removed the sunglasses.

His left eye stared at Terwilliger, unblinking and colorless. His right eye was not there. Instead there was a dark, gaping, scarred hole.

"Jesus," breathed Terwilliger, who had not gone to church in years. "I'd heard about it, but I wasn't sure I believed it. You can have things done, you know. Prosthetics. Not as efficient as what they're doing with limbs, but you could have at least partial sight restored."

"No."

"Why the hell not?"

"Because I deserve it. Because it came from my own stupidity. Because I want the man who did it to me to look into it, and I want it to be the last thing he sees before he goes under the knife for a lobotomy."

What made the words all the more frightening was the way he said it. There was no trace of anger, or fury, or malice. Just a simple, dead-sounding certainty that someone was going to suffer for this.

Quint was the head of special services for the Complex, the organization that had been created to combine the FBI, CIA, and all the other intelligence organizations into one huge network. "Special services" was broadly defined, and Quint was always working to expand it. But apparently someone or something in special services did not want to serve.

Terwilliger had known that something had gone down at the time that it happened, but he hadn't been clear on what. The reports that he received were irritatingly sketchy, and Quint had always made sure to be unavailable to answer full questions. Terwilliger had bided his time in the matter, knowing that when it reached a point where it was important, he would pin Quint down. Now, it seemed, was that time.

"I brought you in here, Quint, because I wanted to assign a matter to the Complex. But first I want you to give me the whole story, now. What the hell happened in Virginia last year?"

Quint paused a moment and then said, "We had an agent. Chuck Simon. Powerful TK. He went renegade—killed a man named Jeffries and then escaped from our Virginia facility, accompanied by a test subject dog. We've had men out after him, and he's surfaced occasionally. His last known location was in Colorado."

"And he was responsible for you losing the eye?"

"In his escape, he shattered the glass windows of a number of our surrounding buildings. He did it as a distracting maneuver, but a piece of glass lodged in my eye and shredded it."

Terwilliger winced. He had heard about that massive accident, but the word that had gotten to him—word that seemed far more believable than the rumors—was that it had been the work of explosives set by terrorists.

He had always been willing to look the other way when it came to Complex activities, but it was becoming clear to him that he was going to have to keep a firmer hand on things, else they could run completely out of control. "I want the full dossier on this man downloaded into my system by this afternoon, Quint. No holding back. No games. I know that the Complex likes to clean up its own messes, and I've always respected that. Hell, I can even appreciate that. But something like this, I have to know."

Terwilliger paused, considering, and then said, "A dog, you said. He escaped with a dog?"

"Yes."

"Oh. All right. Forget it, then. I think I should alert you though—I may have another candidate for your little psychic assassin program. You heard about the attempted assassination of Wyatt Wonder."

"Yes." Slightly annoyed, he added, "You didn't ask for our help on that, I notice. Used freelancers."

"Better that way."

"If it's so much better that way, then why did it fail?"

"We're not sure, but we think it's because of a TK individual, identity unknown. Extent of power unknown. But he's currently with Wyatt Wonder, somewhere in that goddamn park of his. Can you get some people in there?"

"We have."

"What?" Terwilliger was delighted. "I'd heard it was almost impossible."

"It was difficult," admitted Quint. "They have retina scans at the gate, tied in with some sort of central computer system. Whatever sort of setup Wonder has, it's positively mind-boggling. He seems to have the retina patterns of virtually all our people on file. I don't know how he does it, but he does. And he was keeping our people out, the same as he does with anyone who has a serious criminal record. But we managed to sneak a couple of our people in nevertheless. It wasn't easy, but we did it. They can get in at any time. Give the word and we'll send them in to look around."

"Consider the word given," said Terwilliger. "You will undoubtedly want to get your hands on that psionic. And I still want Wonder's head on a platter. Between the two of us, we may be able to accomplish our ends."

Quint started to get up and Terwilliger said, "You sure it was a dog he escaped with?"

"Yes," said Quint, a tad impatiently, "why do you keep asking?"

"Well, this psionic also apparently had an animal with him. But there was no way it was a dog. Our simulations indicate something more on the line of a small bear."

Slowly Quint sat back down again. "A small bear. You mean it was too big to be some normal dog."

"Right. I mean, if this thing were a dog, why it would be the biggest damn dog in the world."

Quint nodded and then said slowly, "Let me tell you about Rommel . . ."

7

THE SPECIAL ELEVATOR opened up right into the castle that let out onto the Main Street. Chuck stood there a moment, taking it all in in amazement.

For one thing, the sun was shining. Shining as he could not recall in ages. He looked up and there it was—clear blue sky, and the warmth of the sun shining down on them. Not a cloud in the sky, and he could not recall a time when there wasn't a cloud in the sky. The pollution that covered the earth like a filthy blanket was just gone.

Impossible.

"Impossible," he said out loud. "I . . . I don't believe it." He drew air into his lungs, and it didn't have the faintly sour aroma to it that the air always had. "The air is clean. The sun is . . ." He looked at Connie incredulously. "The sun is shining. I didn't . . . how can it—?"

"Domed." She pointed, tracing the curve as she pointed. "It's all holographic imagery from cameras mounted in a huge dome that covers the entire park. The air is carefully filtered, cleansed of its pollutants. It never rains here. It's always happy, and it's always safe." She smiled, and she had a beautiful smile. In fact, there was a lot about her that was beautiful, he was starting to realize.

And it had been so long since he had held a woman close, had kissed one. To Chuck, it was important to have a real emotional relationship with a woman before developing anything physical, but with the way his life had been, that hadn't exactly been possible. Relationships or not, Chuck wasn't superhuman—at least, not in that department. All of which went to explain why he was starting to notice little things like her smile, or the curve of her hips or nicely turned tanned leg.

And there was noise. At first he hadn't realized it, so taken had he been by the environmental beauty of the artificial world around him. Now, though, it started to sink in on him, and he looked around at the park as it bustled with people, throbbed with life. All around him were families hustling hither and about, eager to see and do everything, to touch and feel and enjoy it all as they ran along the cobblestone streets that were a nostalgic re-creation of a time no one in the park could remember.

They started to walk down Main Street, and there was the sound of an oom-pah band off to the right as people gathered about to watch. People having a good time, people thriving on the middle-America atmosphere.

Main Street itself was a throwback to early American architecture, with quaintly decorated stores selling everything imaginable. The sunlight (sunlight!) glistened off of elaborate display windows filled either with merchandise the store was carrying, or else special holograms playing out scenes from current Wonder movies.

Here and there children were crying, overwhelmed by the abundance of things to see and do and look at and touch and eat and drink. Here was a family toting shopping bags with Moby Duck's picture emblazoned on the sides, and there was another family having just arrived, making a beeline toward some ride or other they were anxious to leap onto. The air was filled with laughter or crying, of excited chatter everywhere, and it made Chuck feel as if he were in a world that was alive and thriving instead of choking on the product of its own pollution.

Wonderworld was a massive illusion on an unprecedented scale, and Chuck willingly bought into it.

"This place is immense," he said, and was surprised to find that his voice was actually choked up a little.

"Oh, yes," said Connie. She took him by the arm, and he found her touch exciting, even exhilarating. She turned him around and he saw the direction that they'd just come from, the castle from which they had emerged. It was incredibly tall, towers gleaming in the fake rays of the artificial sun image. "The park's divided up into different sections, each one with a specific theme." She pointed off in different directions. "Now over there is Spaceland, that has all sorts of rides and exhibits dealing with our future in space."

"What future in space?" he said in amusement. "They gutted the exploration program years ago in congress."

Her eyes narrowed in amusement. "That's the government. But do you really think that private enterprise is going to let such a resource go untapped? Within ten years, mark my words, there's going to be apartment buildings on Mars."

"I'll be sure to get in my application early," he said.

"Now over there is Imagineland, with all sorts of fantasy-based experiences. Ever ride a unicorn, or go swimming with a mermaid, or get so small you could ride an insect? Imagineland is for you, then. Over there is Joyland—adults only. Child care services are available. Everything you could imagine in the world of erotica."

Chuck coughed politely. "I thought this place was geared for families."

"It is. You'd be amazed at the number of families that got started in Joyland. Stop laughing."

It wasn't easy, and he said so, but forced his laughter to trail off into polite coughing. "Have you got control of yourself now, Chuck?" she asked him, sounding mildly annoyed.

"Yes. Yes, I'm fine."

"Good. Now," and her thoughts disrupted, she ran through the places she'd already pointed out. "Yes. Right. And over there is Pioneerland—go back to the early days of

America, when the country was being explored and settled and everything was new and alive."

He heard a noise that he was hard-pressed to identify. It was some sort of lyrical noise, running up and down scales, and he looked around for the source. Then he spotted them, perched in a nearby tree. "Birds," he said. "And . . . that noise . . . ?"

"Singing. That's birds singing."

He frowned, casting back. "I have a . . . a vague recollection . . . I think I was on a farm, once when I was very little, some sort of a petting zoo or something that my parents took me to. Birds singing." He looked up at them in wonderment. "I never thought I'd see or hear real birds singing again."

"Yes, well . . . you still haven't," she said, her voice dropping to a confidential tone. "You're seeing Animagic."

"What?"

"They're not real birds."

He stared at them in confusion. There was a small brown one with a red front, flapping its little wings every so often and giving out with that lovely tuneless melody. And several more, hopping from branch to branch. "They're holograms?"

"No. As I said, they're Anigmaics. The old science fiction term would be androids, but you can't trademark androids. Animagic, Animagics, and Animagicians—the fellows who make them—are all trademarks of the Wonder Films Company. So watch it, fella," she held up a mock-scolding finger.

He took a step closer, watching the birds move. "I can't believe it," he said. "They're so sophisticated . . ."

"Oh, that's nothing," she said, stepping next to him, and for some reason he found the closeness of her very distracting. "They're actually pretty simple, as Animagics go. Very limited memory. If you stand here long enough, you'll see that their flitting about actually runs a pattern. Preprogrammed as to what branches they go to, what notes they sing—they even turn their heads on cue. They're very primitive in comparison to what Wonder Company is capable of producing."

"And what are they capable of?"

At that moment they heard excitement as from all around them, children's voices went up in cheers and giggles and screams of excitement. The kids went stampeding past, and Chuck looked around in confusion. "What—?"

The children, in their cries, answered his question. "Moby! Moby!"

Sure enough, there was Moby Duck, in his more nebbish form. Chuck looked on in amazement as, far bigger than life—well over six feet tall, in fact—Moby Duck waddled down the street, hugging and embracing the children, waving and posing for pictures. Most children swarmed around him like ants, although some of the smaller ones sobbed in fear. Parents of these smaller ones didn't know what to do, because the kids had seemed so primed to meet the duck of their dreams, had talked about nothing else the entire drive to Wonderworld. Yet here he was now, in the flesh—well, feathers—and their kids hung back in fear.

"The really little kids never know how to react," Connie commented to Chuck, her mouth twitching in sympathy for the beleaguered parents. "The older kids buy into the fantasy of their hero come to life. But the smaller ones are trying to reconcile a world where this huge, hideously mutated adult-sized figure is lumbering toward them, and they don't know what to do."

"Except cry," said Chuck.

"Except cry," she agreed.

They took in the excitement of the crowd for a brief time longer, Chuck thriving on it. He had seen some measure of this when he had been with the circus, but it had been a different environment. With the circus, a place where he had hidden from the Complex, it had been an attempt to divert people for a few hours from their humdrum, even dreary towns, by attempting to entertain them with the two-bit acts and carny games the circus had to offer. In many ways, particularly with the steady, unchanging gray skies hanging over everything, it had been as depressing as it was entertaining. Perhaps it even leaned a bit more on the depressing side.

But here there was an entire package. Birds singing, sun shining, everyone happy and joyful, standing next to the outsize duck and posing for pictures snapped with holocams. It was a carefully manufactured experience.

Chuck remembered reading the occasional criticism of Wonderworld, taking it to task for being deliberately unrealistic, for being too commercial, for being exploitive of people's deepest wishes and most nostalgic dreams and giving it to them in easily purchasable packages. Moby Duck, it was argued, was not a beloved childhood symbol, but instead a representative of all that was greedy and avaricious. Moby Duck, it was argued, was an overwhelming bully who stomped on whatever got in his way, just as his creators did.

Perhaps the critics had a point, Chuck reasoned. But the simple fact was that he didn't care. No one cared. Commercial? Crass? Money-grubbing? So what. Everyone was having too good a time to worry about labels being tacked on.

Chuck felt an arm snake through his and looked down at Connie, who was smiling at him now. At first she had come across as the utterly standoffish secretary, determined to keep him at arm's length. And, truth to tell, he wasn't sure if he wanted to be much closer than that. But out here, in the park, watching the joyful families, watching everyone have such a good time, it made Chuck want to join in somehow. But he had no child to shove forward toward the obliging duck, and he had no one with whom he could share his general feelings of peace and happiness . . . or did he? That was now the question he was asking himself, looking down at the charming Mexican woman.

He still had trouble getting impressions of her, but damn, she smelled good. Rommel had been right, she did have a pleasant scent, wherever it was coming from. Although Chuck was not about to stick his nose between her legs— certainly not on a first date, at any rate.

She squeezed his arm briefly and smiled. "Where would you like to go first?"

All of the various parts of the park sounded interesting, and he was that much more astounded when he heard himself say, "How about Joyland?"

He was amazed at himself. How could he have suggested that? Good Lord, that was for lovers. For people with a relationship. From what he'd heard about the place, it was certainly totally inappropriate. He wouldn't blame her if she slapped him or looked at him with repugnance or—

"Okay."

He turned slowly and looked at her. There was genuine interest in her eyes.

"You, uh," he said hesitantly, "you don't have to, of course; we could try something else, or—"

She laughed and squeezed his arm a bit more tightly. "Come on, Chuck, for heaven's sake. Come join the twenty-first century."

"Uh . . . well, sure, I guess."

She seemed amazed. "Look, we don't have to go on any of the rides if you don't want to. We can just look around. Whatever makes you feel comfortable. That's my job, to put you at ease."

That stopped him, and he turned and took her by the shoulders. "Are you playing along because you want to, or because it's your job to do it?" he said.

Her eyes narrowed and her already dark cheeks flushed. "My job description doesn't extend to being a whore," she said, "if that's what you mean."

Immediately he felt contrite, and she turned away from him as he said quickly, "Look, I'm sorry, I didn't mean to—"

That was when the cries of laughter from all around them turned to screams of terror.

"They're killing Moby!"

Chuck spun and looked on in confusion as people were running all over, crying out and shouting for help. All about him was pandemonium.

Killing Moby? What the hell was going on?

Security guards ran past him, looking bizarre with their combination of side arms and cheerful duck faces on their uniforms. He tried to make out the origin of the problem——and found it.

Three young men had Snapped.

The drug of choice this year, as it had been the previous year and the year before that, was Snap. Unlike the old days when drugs were available for money, most drug traffic these days was done through the black market for barter. But how the drugs were acquired was not nearly so important as that they were acquired at all.

Snap was introduced into the system any one of a number of ways, in any of a half-dozen different forms. Some types of Snap merely reduced you to utter stupefication in a matter of minutes, letting you forget the miserable shape the world was in and instead contemplate the cosmic fascination of the inside of your eyelids.

There was another type that killed one time in six. Its street name was Russian Roulette.

Another gave you the incredible sensation you were flying, the concept being that you could go soaring above the polluted haze that was the earth and instead revel in the glory of the atmosphere, wherever that might be. The majority of people who took headers out of windows these days were in the throes of that particular drug.

Another supposedly expanded your field of thought, and so on, and so on.

And one was called Time Bomb.

Time Bomb didn't hit you all at once. Indeed, the major kick for Time Bomb was the sense of breathless anticipation. Wondering when the drug was going to kick in. On average it was around six hours, although Time Bomb was curious in that if a group of Bombardiers were together and one of them went off, the others would invariably be set off too.

Time Bomb sent you into a flurry of activity. As your brain tripped off into the ozone, your body would be seized in a spasm of berserker strength and you would quite simply go nuts. Bombardiers thought it was marvelous, the idea of freeing their bodies from the constraints of normal human strength and turning into unstoppable juggernauts. When you came down from Time Bomb, the overwhelming imperative was to get some more so that you could continue to have that same feeling of breathless anticipation.

Since there were so many variations of Snap, the overall catch phrase for someone who was using it, no matter what the form, was a Snapper. And someone under the influence had Snapped.

The Time Bomb had kicked in for the young men a good four hours after they had entered the gates of Wonderworld. It was their first experience with the drug, and they had never been arrested, so the retina scans had revealed no reason whatsoever to keep them out. Now, of course, it was too late for anything except damage control.

They had no weapons—fortunately the scanners at the gate were too efficient to allow anything like that. But when you were a Bombardier, you didn't need any weapon other than your own body.

Nevertheless, one of the Bombardiers had fashioned a weapon—his belt, which he had yanked out of the loops and was using to throttle poor Moby Duck. Unlike his animated counterpart, Moby couldn't transform into a massive, unstoppable engine of destruction. Instead the helpless duck twisted and turned, the belt effectively garroting across his throat.

A half-dozen guards were rushing forward, their weapons out, but they were reluctant to fire because there were too many people around. The Bombardiers had gone off at the worst possible time, right in the middle of an admiring throng, and it was the devil's own time getting near them.

The Bombardiers, however, did not care in the least about innocents. The three of them looked almost the same under the drug's influence—their hair was disheveled, standing out as if they'd stuck their fingers in sockets. Their eyes were wild, their mouths twisted into drooling smears across their faces.

One of them grabbed up the nearest object at hand, which happened to be a little girl, aged six. He ripped her from the grasp of her mother who was trying to retreat. The mother screamed and then was shoved backward against her will by the stampede of the crowd trying to get away. Even though the crowd obviously outnumbered the Bombardiers, no one wanted to reckon with the strength that the drug gave its users.

The lunatic swung the little girl up into his face, snarling and chuckling and drooling at her. The child shrieked, a high, terrified scream, and the Bombardier drew back his arm and hurled her.

She arched over the desperate, outstretched hands of the guards, tumbling end over end, and then, quite without warning, she started to slow. She drifted toward the ground, like a feather on a zephyr, and a guard caught her and held her close whispering to her that everything was going to be all right.

"Stop them!" came the yells of the guards, and one of them managed to get close enough to fire a bolt at the Bombardier who had thrown the little girl.

None of the weapons they carried fired something as destructive or final as bullets. Instead they were loaded with bolts, minigenerators that penetrated the skin and, a split second later, sent through the body of the victim enough voltage to stop a charging rhino.

It did not stop the Bombardier. He shook in his tracks, his body trembling in a spasm of pain under the shock that his system received. But the information telling him that he was being overwhelmed never reached his brain, and because of that, he didn't know enough to fall down. Instead he twisted and shook under the charge, and as soon as the bolt had run out of juice, he staggered forward and grabbed at the guard who had shot him.

He snapped the man's arm.

The guard shrieked, going down, blood fountaining out and covering the nice, tidy cobblestones of Main Street.

The Bombardier who was straddling Moby Duck twisted his belt once more, and Moby's head twisted around at an impossible angle, a loud *crack* sounding even above the noise of screams and shouts and hysteria that filled an air that had, only moments before, known only singing birds and laughing children.

The guards fell back, trying to get clear shots with their weapons—weapons that had already proven useless—and Chuck leaped forward and yanked the Bombardier off the back of Moby Duck.

The Bombardier fell, feathers clutched in his hand, and he staggered to his feet and came straight at Chuck. Moby Duck fell to the ground, unmoving, but Chuck had no time to give the mangled mallard even the briefest of glances. He barely, in fact, had time to strike a defensive aikido stance before the Bombardier was upon him.

His strength was frightening, but aikido wasn't about strength versus strength. It was about using strength against itself, and this Chuck did. The Bombardier attacked with no grace or artistry, merely manic power, and that meant little or nothing to Chuck. Chuck spun in between the outstretched arms, grabbed the right one, set himself, and twisted, adding the force of his own muscles and his TK power behind it. The Bombardier slammed down into the ground, facefirst.

There was the sound of ripping cloth and Chuck suddenly found himself holding a sleeve. The Bombardier got to his feet, and that was when another arm closed around Chuck's throat. Another one of the Bombardiers had him from behind, in a devastating choke hold.

Chuck didn't panic. Didn't come close. Instead he grabbed the wrist of the arm that was around him, twisting it. Even in the mind-rising circumstance of his drugged state, the Bombardier couldn't keep the grip. Chuck brought the arm straight up over his head, his feet moving quickly, and as his body spun he hurled the Bombardier forward. The Bombardier smashed into the one who had just gotten up and they both went down in a tangle of arms and legs.

Behind him the third Bombardier was shaking off the guards who were trying to hold him down. He was enough of a distance away, and the situation was right, that Chuck could subtly use his power. He mentally envisioned a fist and slammed it down on the Bombardier, but it seemed as if the guards had done it as they shoved him to the ground, binding his arms and legs in unbreakable plastic and metal-reinforced ties.

He turned his attention back to the first two—a moment too late, for he was slammed from behind and sent hurtling to the ground. Chuck cracked his head against the cobblestone and he felt one of them on top of him. He tried to stagger to his feet, only managed to get to one knee, and there was an arm to his right about to grab his throat. He snatched at the arm and twisted, trying to push the arm back. "I don't . . . want to hurt you . . ." he gasped out, but the Bombardier wasn't listening, instead gibbering insanely into his ear.

Chuck angled himself around now, and he was chest-to-chest with his assailant, shoving the arm away. The Bombardier was pushing forward, heedless, demented, and Chuck grunted from the strain, "Stop . . . please . . ."

A second or two more and the man's arm would be broken. Then the Bombardier brought his other hand around and grabbed Chuck's throat and Chuck knew he had no choice.

And that was when the Bombardier's head caved in.

Even that calamitous occurrence took a few moments to register on the Bombardier, and then he keeled over. His frontal lobe was now doing a respectable impression of his rear lobe, and he hit the ground, unmoving, blood beginning to well from his ears.

Chuck looked up and saw Connie standing over him, horrified, a large cobblestone in her hands that, Chuck presumed, had been knocked loosed during the fight. There was blood and some gore on it, and Connie was staring at it as if it had just magically appeared in her hands, all besmeared with human residue.

And behind her loomed the last of the Bombardiers.

Chuck was ready to let caution be damned and just mentally smash the bastard down, but at that moment several more guards body-slammed him to the ground, and as accelerated as his strength was, it wasn't enough to cope with the men who were covering him.

Chuck rose unsteadily to his feet and went straight to Connie. She was trembling, still holding the stone. "You all right?" he asked.

She didn't nod, didn't shake her head, didn't do anything.

"Come on," he said gently, and pried the stone from her hands. He dropped it to the ground, where it fell with a clunk and then rolled a short distance away.

They started to walk away and the guards, recognizing Connie Lopez, did nothing to stop them.

Within five minutes the area would be completely cleaned up. The body would be gone, and the living Bombardiers locked away until they dried out, at which time they would be ejected from the park. The street would be hosed down, the cobblestone replaced, the upset customers given special dinners, souvenirs, a free week's stay at the Wonderworld Deluxe Hotel, and lifetime passes for them and their descendants. Within an hour no one would know that there had been any problem, and there would be no complaints, no recriminations, no difficulties of any kind in this, the Safest Place in the World.

For that was the magic of Wonder.

8

CHUCK STEPPED OFF the elevator, one arm around Connie, in time to hear a massive roaring and barking, accompanied by the sounds of a number of voices raised in what sounded like utter confusion, fear, and fright. There was the brief sound of a sharp zapping noise that Chuck immediately recognized as being some sort of electric prod. And he knew who was on the receiving end.

Connie forgotten, he dashed from the elevator into the corridor and hung a right. There was Rommel, turning this way and that, surrounded by four extremely tentative-looking guards. Three of them were wielding prods, and the fourth was dangling a choke loop nearby Rommel's head, clearly in hope of snagging him.

Chuck was almost tempted to let them continue to try, because even if they'd snagged Rommel's head, the huge animal would have managed to yank the rod from his momentary captor's hands with little to no difficulty. But Chuck wasn't going to just stand around and let all this happen anyway.

"What's going on?!" he shouted. "What do you think you're doing to my dog!"

The men stopped, clearly relieved. "He'd gone nuts, sir!

He was running all over the place, smashing into things, knocking people over."

Rommel looked up at Chuck as the man approached. *I was looking for you*, said Rommel sourly. *I knew you were in trouble.*

"And you couldn't find a way out," said Chuck.

Yeah. They have something in the air here, kills the scents. I couldn't follow the way you'd gone out, and I couldn't get out to just home in on your thoughts.

"Sorry." Chuck smiled, kneeling down and rubbing Rommel's head.

Yeah, well, you shouldn't have gone walking off.

"I'm said I'm sorry."

You should be.

Chuck stood and looked at the guards apologetically. "Sorry, guys. It won't happen again."

The guards looked at one another with a mixture of uncertainty and relief. "Really, it'll be fine," Chuck said again, and slowly they walked away, casting nervous glances over their shoulders as if concerned that Rommel would take another shot at them.

Where were you?

"Upstairs," said Chuck. "You wouldn't believe the place. Blue skies, birds, music, and crazed drug addicts."

Any food?

"Oh, yeah."

Sounds good.

"Connie saved my life." It wasn't entirely true. He could have handled things himself—indeed, was in the middle of so doing—but it sounded good. For that matter, it was curiously important to Chuck that Rommel like Connie. He didn't know why, or what the point of it was. He knew that Rommel had never warmed to Dakota, and although he was reluctant to admit it to himself, that was part of what had hampered his feelings about her. So he wanted Rommel to like Connie so that . . .

So that what?

He wasn't sure if he could, or wanted to, complete that thought.

"It was nothing," Connie said, still looking a bit dazed.

Rommel looked her up and down. *Her? The one who smells funny?*

"Right. Her."

Just luck.

Chuck frowned at that. Dammit, why did Rommel have to have such an attitude problem? Well . . . maybe it was because he was a dog. Certainly that was a major contributing factor.

Then the elevator doors opened again, and several men and women in different color uniforms from the guards came running out, carrying two stretchers. On the first was a softly moaning guard, his injured arm immobilized. He was immediately carted out of sight. In the middle of the other stretcher was none other than Moby Duck, his head twisted, his eyes wide open, his body unmoving.

"One side!" the stretcher carriers were shouting, and Chuck obediently stepped over toward the edge of the hallway. He didn't know, sadly, what they were rushing for. Whoever that poor actor was inside that costume, he was unquestionably dead. His head had been all but torn from his shoulders.

The duck's eyes caught Chuck's sad expression, and to Chuck's utter shock, the fouled-up fowl gave him a slow thumbs-up. Moby kept the arm raised as he was hurried off down the hallway.

"My God, Chuck, you look white as a sheet," Connie was saying, and he realized that she'd been speaking to him for a few moments and he hadn't been focusing in on her.

"He's—he's alive," Chuck stammered out.

"No he's not," Connie replied.

"But—but he . . . but I saw . . ."

"Oh. Oh! You thought he was an actor," Connie said, understanding now. "No, no, you poor, confused person. Remember when you were asking about more complicated Animagics? He was one."

Chuck was speechless for a moment. "You mean—you mean he wasn't really . . ."

"A person. No. He's a machine. State of the art,

incredibly crafted, but a machine. I'm sorry if you didn't realize that. It gave you a fright, huh?"

He started to laugh, gasping in relief. "I just . . . I . . . gods!" He was still incredulous. "Yeah, you had me completely fooled, I admit it. It didn't occur to me that he was anything else other than a person. That is really the most remarkable thing I've ever seen. A machine? Really?"

"Really." She nodded.

"But how are you doing?" he asked her, suddenly remembering.

"You mean, how am I doing considering that I just killed somebody? Ah, well"—and she forced a ragged smile— "I'm going to come down with the dry heaves in about a half hour or so. But other than that, I'm doing just fine."

"I really appreciate what you did," he said, touching her shoulder. "I—"

But she brushed his hand away and said softly, "Not now. Okay, Chuck? Just . . . I really want to be by myself for a while. I hope you understand."

He nodded. It was a hideous position to be in, having taken the life of one in order to save the life of another. After all, had not he done that himself? To save the lives of Connie and Wonder? For that matter, out of a misplaced sense of vengeance over a year ago? Oh, yes . . . he most certainly did understand. All too well.

He stood there and watched her go, wishing he could do something but not knowing what.

A shadow cast itself over him, and he turned and looked up at the imposing form of Wyatt Wonder. "I hear I owe you yet again," said Wonder. "It's amazing I've been able to survive as long as I have before you turned up."

"If it hadn't been me, it would have been something else," said Chuck.

"Perhaps. Chuck, my friend, there's something I need to show you." Rommel rumbled a warning and Wyatt added smoothly, "Of course, feel free to invite your little friend along."

"Rommel generally always considers himself invited,"

replied Chuck. "That way he never has to feel as if he's barging in somewhere."

"Very sound," Wyatt said sagely. "Very sound. Come along, then." He patted Chuck on the back with enough controlled strength that Chuck got a brief impression of just how strong his towering host really was. He followed Wonder down the hallway.

"I'll tell you right now," said Chuck, matching his stride with some effort to Wonder's, "If you try and bring me into another room and depart, I'm leaving immediately. I'm not about to expose myself to another barrage of promotional material."

"That's quite understandable," said Wonder. "I submit that if you weren't feeling so under the weather, you wouldn't have had as much difficulty with my initial presentation."

"I would disagree with that," said Chuck. "I think if I'd been in the pink of health it would still have been a bit much to handle."

"Pure advertising" was the sad reply. "A lost art in this homogenized, government-sponsored, government-controlled time in which we live. Here we go." And he gestured for Chuck to enter what appeared to be a screening room. Chuck did so, with Rommel staying outside, just behind Wonder, giving out a silent message of warning to Wonder. Wonder, aware of Rommel's positioning, picked up on it. "Your companion seems reluctant to enter the room until I do," he observed.

"He wants to make damned sure you enter," Chuck acknowledged. "So do I. You'll find that, on most issues, Rommel and I are of the same mind."

"How convenient," said Wonder as he entered, followed by Rommel. "Choose a seat. Any one you'd like," and he gestured around the small theater. "This won't take long, really. I want to just show you a few pictures and see if you can identify them."

Chuck shrugged and sat in the third row from the front. Wonder sat just behind him and to the right. Rommel contented himself with lying on the carpeted aisle.

"Lights," called out Wonder, and when the lights went out Wonder continued, "First slide."

A man in cobalt-blue sunglasses appeared on the screen. The screen had a three-dimensional effect, making it appear as if the man were really in the room with them—a feeling that Chuck could most definitely have done without.

"Quint," said Chuck immediately. "Big man in the Complex. My original 'recruiter,' until I discovered just how insidious the entire outfit really was."

"That's what I like about you, Chuck," said Wonder amiably. "Your perpetual high degree of moral outrage. Yes, we had him identified as Quint too. He had a recent meeting with this man," and another picture flashed up on the screen. "Know him?"

Chuck stared at the picture. "Nooooo. Should I?"

"Not really. Name's Terwilliger. Right-hand man to the president."

"Any particular reason I should know the president's right-hand man?" asked Chuck.

"Because any man should know his enemies. And Terwilliger is definitely your enemy, make no mistake about that. Our government is not stupid. Irritating, autocratic, totalitarian, yes. But not stupid. If they figure out a way to connect you with your saving me, they're going to want to nail you as badly as they want to get me."

"I assure you, Wyatt, I'm already low on their popularity list."

"Okay. Now this next man, we're fuzzy on. But we have reason to believe that Quint's assigned him to come out here and try to find out what's what. You know him?"

Another picture came onto the 3-D screen. A pleasant-looking man, with a narrow face and very relaxed air about him.

Rommel lifted his head and growled before Chuck could even say anything. Wonder noticed and raised an eyebrow. "Your associate seems to know him."

"Oh, yes," said Chuck tightly. "He knows him. So do I. Name's Reuel Beutel."

"Who is he?"

Chuck turned to look over his shoulder. "He's what they wanted me to become."

In another country . . .

El presidente was inspecting his troops. They stood in line, elbow to elbow, their rifles held smartly across their chests, mounted bayonets sparkling and cleansed of recent bloodstains. Their uniforms were crisp and neatly pressed, their looks somewhat glassy but determined.

The soldiers had recently put down yet another rebellion by the unhappy citizenry. Each battle had been more difficult than the one before as civil unrest grew greater and greater with each passing month. There had been talk that the United States might secretly be behind the uprisings, goading the people into revolt since they themselves were too cowardly to fund a revolution outright. Yes, cowardly and weak were the American bastards, and afraid.

El presidente chuckled as he walked past his men. *His* men, who would lay down their lives for him at his merest whim. It was not a privilege that he could take lightly. He had not liked having to send his men out to combat the populace, for this was truly brother against brother. There was, however, no choice, and his soldiers understood that. Understood that and lived with it.

It was all a deliberate show of strength. Citizens lined their balconies, peered out of their windows, got as close as the barricades and human blockades of soldiers would allow them to. What they were seeing was their presidente, letting the country know that he was unafraid, that he was protected, that he was in total and complete charge.

Before, when the soldiers had come marching out onto the streets that just two days ago had been red with blood, the populace had cheered wildly for them. They had to. The rebels had all been driven back into the jungles, there to be hunted down sooner or later. Those who had been captured had been publicly executed. All in all, it was neither a good time nor a good place to be suspected of being in sympathy with rebels. That was a good way to be shot. So people cheered instead.

El presidente stopped in front of one soldier. The others around him were looking straight ahead with fixed, determined gazes. But this man looked just the least saddened, for reasons that were obvious and yet should not, could not, be allowed to continue. He regarded the soldier and, with one eyebrow raised, said, "Do you respect your presidente?"

The soldier snapped to with pleasing promptness. "Yes, sir."

"Show your respect."

El presidente expected a brisk salute.

Instead the soldier's rifle suddenly swung around as if it had taken on a life of its own. He gripped it tighter, trying to get control over this weapon that seemed determined to leap from his grasp.

The bayonette rammed into el presidente in the solar plexus, just under the rib cage, angling upward and slicing through the dictator's heart and, for good measure, cutting over and slicing through his right lung. As blood from the country's leader flowed, the bayonette continued downward, dragging the hapless soldier's rifle behind it, slicing downward across the stomach that the dictator had been slapping in self-satisfaction just that very morning, admiring the firmness it still possessed in middle age. The firm skin slowed down the knife not at all and it cut downward to his belt buckle, where it stopped.

The soldier stood there, frozen in horror and shock, as most of the internal organs of his leader poured out onto his nicely polished boots. The entire thing had taken not more than a few seconds, and el presidente had not had a chance to say anything in the way of last words. (Although later on Famous Last Words would be made up for him that, roughly translated, would be "Ah, I am slain, on the eve of my triumph!")

The dictator slid off the bayonette and fell, blood gurgling in his throat, and truthfully he was dead before he even hit the ground. He had company moments later, for the appalled and nauseated soldier was shot through the head on the spot before he even had the chance to try to explain that it hadn't been his idea. That the rifle had simply come to life and decided to stab el presidente all on its own. It is doubtful that this rather meager explanation would have carried much weight, despite the fact that it happened to be the truth.

All around now was confusion, screaming and shouting, wailing that was a mixture of lamentation and thanksgiving.

And, in an overlooking balcony, a pleasant appearing man looked down upon it all, serene and content, and turned and went back into his room. Once inside he picked up the phone and dialed a number that he knew would be answered on the first ring.

"This is Beutel," he said, lighting up another cigarette.

"Yes?" said the voice on the other end.

"Weee-llll," said Beutel, in that way he had of dragging out one-syllable words, using that aw-shucks midwestern twang of his, "if you boys'd sent me out on this in the first place, we could have saved ourselves a whole lot of time."

The noise of the confused and hysterical crowd was beginning to be bothersome, and Beutel ordered the doors leading to the balcony to close so that he could concentrate. They obediently did so, and the noise lessened slightly.

"Good thing you're done," said the voice. "Quint wants you back. Just sent orders down. You'll never guess·who they think they've got a line on."

Beutel was silent a moment, watching the smoke from the cigarette. "You're not shitting me now, are ya, son?"

"No, sir," said the voice with relish. "Simon."

"Psiiii-Man." He smiled and raised his right hand. It closed into a fist with a metallic clack, gleaming in the dim lighting of the room. "Now that is the best news I've heard in quite, quite some time."

9

"Hssst. Hey, Wes? You asleep?"

The old man slowly opened his eyes, which, at his age, was always something of an accomplishment. After all, every day you were never certain if it was going to be your last, or if you were going to wake up the following morning.

"Didn't think so. C'mon, Wes. C'mon. Let's play."

He half propped himself up in bed and peered in confusion at the source of the voice. There, leaning against the door frame, was Moby Duck. Not that huge Animagic creature that his son had constructed. But the actual Moby, the cartoon Moby, as real and alive as the cartoons had appeared in any of those films that were combinations of animation and live action.

Wes smiled. "How you doing, Moby?" His voice was like a ghostly thing in his chest.

"Fine. I'm doing fine. Wanna come play?"

"Can't."

"Why not?" Moby waddled over to him and hopped lightly up onto the bed. "What'sa matter, anyway? You look crummy." He opened Wes's mouth wide and looked in. "Hello!" he shouted, and his voice echoed back at him.

"Hello. Hello. Hello." His neck distended comically as he stuck his head down into Wes's throat, then pulled it back out and looked at him, his face distorted into an unpleasant expression. "Pizza with onions tonight, Wes? Criminey. The stuff that you have lining the inside of your stomach looks like Jersey beach at low tide. Truly appalling." He took Wes's head by either side and looked at it carefully. "You've really let yourself go since you made me, guy."

"Gotten old," said Wes. "Old and tired and sick."

"But you couldn't have. I'm not old."

"I made you to last," Wes said, smiling. "I gave you that. Back"—and his head dropped back into the pillow of his stark white bed—"back in the days when everything was small. A small company, that's all I wanted. Make small movies, give people a good time. That's all that it was supposed to be. Not this megalith. Not this giant thing that ate every other form of entertainment. That's not what I wanted."

Moby sat back and stared at Wes with upraised eyebrows, a fairly effective trick considering he didn't have any. "You talk like you know what's going on. The guys out there"—and he chucked a nonexistent thumb in the direction of the door—"they all think you don't know what's happening these days."

"They think that," said Wes. "They can think that. I want them to think that. I want them to think lots of things." He coughed once, a phlegm-filled hacking wheeze, and he patted his chest a couple times to pull himself back together. When he looked up at Moby again, it was with a canny, conniving look. "But only I know. Heh. Only I know what's really going on."

"And what's really going on, Wes?"

Wes grinned craftily. "Can you keep a secret?"

Moby leaned forward. "Sure."

"Well . . . so can I."

"Arrrhhhhh!!" Moby pitched back, clutching his head with his feathery arms. "Nailed by one of the oldest gags in the world. How could I have fallen for that? How? How?"

" 'Cause you're a cartoon," Wes informed him airily. "And cartoons never learn a damned thing. You think Pistol Pete or Wall-Eyed Pike would fall for the same gags you pull on them, over and over again, in every cartoon, if they learned from their past mistakes? How long do you think Ozzie Ostrich would stay one step ahead of Nick Jackalson if that stupid jackal would only realize, just once, that those stupid Acme products always backfire? Every single cartoon we ever produced had one simple theme to it— predator versus prey. And every single time the prey always escapes because the predator never gets smart. That's how"—he raised a hand and pointed at Moby—"that's how cartoons are different from real life. Because in real life, the predators generally get whatever they're after. Because predators are evil and prey is good, and prey never, never fully learns never to be trusting. And predators . . . why, they know that from the start."

Moby nodded slowly. "You're full of big advice tonight, aren't you, Wes? Look . . . you want to come out for a while? All the other guys are waiting outside."

And indeed, sticking their heads in now were a plethora of other characters, waving and cheering and calling Wes's name.

"I don't know," said Wes. "Maybe I . . ."

At that moment he heard the brisk footfalls of the nurse. All the other characters except Moby promptly sought hiding places, and Moby watched them with obvious amusement.

The nurse came in, a slim, attractive young woman, and Moby looked her up and down. As she spoke, telling Wes it was time for his medication and my, wasn't he looking fit this evening, Moby mimicked all her movements and tone with such accuracy that Wes was hard-pressed not to go into fits of convulsive laughter.

"My, you're in a good mood tonight," she observed, not noticing at all the animated duck standing next to her, batting impossibly huge eyelashes in imitation. Wes nodded mutely, not trusting himself to speak, and after taking his medication he watched the nurse go. Moby walked behind her, sashaying his hips in ludicrous imitation.

Then Moby turned and shook his head. "What're you staying in this dump for, anyhow?"

"Beats the hell out of me," agreed Wes. He yawned widely.

"Come on," said Moby urgently, taking Wes by the fingers and pulling with all his strength, which didn't amount to much. "Really. I'll show you a good place, a wonderful place. The kinds of places you didn't think existed anymore outside of that overblown park overhead that your son distorted."

He yawned widely. "I'll think about it," but every word was an effort as the medication kicked in.

"Don't think about it, Wes," pleaded Moby, as he felt himself starting to dissolve. "Just do it." But it was too late. Wes Wonder snored noisily, and Moby Duck faded out.

Chuck sat in his room reading. What a curious thing, he realized, considering that at his fingertips was a dazzling array of virtually any movie that Wonder Films had made within the last thirty years. They sat there, waiting to be played, his voice command the only thing required to activate the large 3-D screen opposite his bed.

His room was extremely ornate—rooms, actually. There was a sitting room with deep, plush red carpeting, deep couches that you could sink into, and recliner chairs—Lord, did he used to love recliner chairs. A pleasant recollection from childhood when one of his favorite things in the world was a recliner chair that was in the living room of his grandfather's house. He'd play in the thing for hours, sliding it open and closed, open and closed. He had tried it a couple times now, but somehow the old thrill just wasn't there anymore.

The adjoining room was the bedroom, where the screen was set up. The bed was insanely ornate, a four-poster with an elaborate canopy, and matching quilt, dust ruffles, pillowcases—the whole bit. Chuck had always considered beds to be purely functional, not fashion statements. Still, it was interesting for a change of pace. And at least his room was more elaborate than Rommel's, though not by much . . .

He was surprised to realize that he actually missed having Rommel at his side all the time.

He supposed he couldn't blame the dog. Being thrown into luxurious surroundings such as these were sure to turn the head of virtually anyone or anything. Four-legged or no. Still, he wondered what Rommel was up to . . .

And then there came a soft knocking at the door.

He tried to sense if there was danger involved, but somehow—despite the old saying—danger rarely seemed to come knocking at his door. Instead it usually just kicked the door down, spraying bullets in front of it and leaving destruction in its wake. Danger was many things, but rarely, if ever, polite.

"Yes?" he called.

The door slid open and a female figure was silhouetted in the dimness of the corridor lighting—dim since the underground passageways were brought down in order to simulate the falling of night. Chuck caught a brief glimpse of a tight white gown that he imagined, from the glossy texture and the way it hugged curves, to be made of silk.

He cleared his throat, already feeling as if there were too much blood in his body, and he said, "Excuse me," as the door hissed shut. "Connie, is that you?"

She did not cross the room so much as glide, her footfalls like a whisper. "Yes," she said softly, "it's me. Who else would it be?"

"I'm not sure. And when I'm not sure"—and he cleared his throat yet again—"I tend to get nervous."

"Oh, that's sad." She was much closer now. She settled on the far end of the bed, springs creaking softly under her. "That's sad," she repeated. "A man like you, a brave man, a strong man—getting upset and nervous just because there's a woman in your room."

She placed a hand on his leg and he felt the hairs on the back of his neck rise. And that wasn't the only thing rising.

He slowly withdrew his leg from her, tucking it under him and trying to resist the sudden urge to paw the ground or bray at the moon. He wished Rommel were nearby.

Rommel! God, a gorgeous woman was putting overt moves on him and he was becoming nostalgic for the company of his pooch. What the hell was happening to him?

"Connie," he said, surprised at the unsteadiness of his voice. "This isn't right. You shouldn't be here." He didn't sound convincing, even to himself.

"If this is about that remark earlier, don't worry about it," her words came to him from the darkness. He was beginning to be able to make out her face, floating in front of him. "I was pressured, you were pressured. It was difficult for both of us."

"Yes! Yes, exactly," said Chuck, sounding a bit too enthusiastic. "And I'm worried that your being here . . . that you're not thinking straight. You see? That you're still laboring under the stress of the moment."

"The moment's passed." Her hand had now returned, to rest on his thigh. "It's time to move on to new moments."

Blood was pounding inside his head, and he was becoming dizzy just from the intoxicating nearness of her. "You have to understand . . ."

"What? What do I have to understand?"

"I don't like to rush into relationships. Sex is," and he coughed. God, he couldn't even remember the last time he'd even said the word, much less done the deed. "Sex is something that should be special."

"Are you saying that sex with me wouldn't be special?" There was no anger in her voice, only teasing.

"No. No, I'm not saying that at all. I'm sure it would be very special. But—but I don't know anything about you, really."

"I find you attractive. Isn't that all you need to know?"

"No! I mean . . ." He was having trouble keeping track of the conversation, and the extreme twitching that he was feeling below the waist wasn't helping. His heart was pounding against his rib cage like hammers on a xylophone. "There has to be more to a relationship than that."

"Can't we just make love and build the relationship from there?" With her other hand she gently stroked his face, and the nearness of her was staggering. The room temperature felt as if it had skyrocketed. "You're trembling."

"I'm not," he said quickly. "I'm just thrilled . . ."

"Thrilled?"

". . . with the idea that you want to . . ."

"Want to what?"

". . . get better acquainted."

"Is that what I want?" She sounded as if she didn't know what to make of any of this.

"Yes. Yes, Connie, you see . . . we should talk."

She sat back, her hands folded on her lap. Her voice was thick with amusement. "What do you want to talk about?"

"Uhmmm . . . sports?"

"Sports?" She sounded incredulous.

"Yes. Sports," he said eagerly. "What types of sports are your favorite?"

"Horizontal."

He tried a different tack. "What's your favorite part of sports."

"Scoring."

He winced, and she said helpfully, "Do you want to discuss various positions? Wide receiver, or . . ."

"No, that's quite okay. Look . . . Connie . . . this is really making me uncomfortable. I'm trying to be honest with you. You sitting there in that nightgown . . . I just . . ."

"Okay." She patted his head. "I understand."

She stood up and Chuck breathed a sigh of relief. The sigh caught in his throat, though, as he heard the soft rushing of cloth when Connie slid the nightgown up and over her head. She settled back down on the bed, and even in the dimness, he could see she was nude.

To point out that was not what he had meant seemed more than useless.

* * *

Rommel, dozing lightly, abruptly came to full wakefulness.

The door had slid open and she had entered. Rommel's eyes opened wide, his ears perked up.

He caught the scent of her immediately, and a low growl of pleasure sounded deep in his throat.

She was large . . . not as large as he, of course. Still, not bad for a female German shepherd.

She, for her part, seemed impressed by him. They circled each other slowly, sniffing each other out. Her fur was a much lighter brown than Rommel's, but it had a glossy sheen to it that Rommel found extremely enticing. Not that he needed much enticement.

He barked once, sharply, and she responded in kind. Yes, there was definite room for communication here. His tail stood straight out, as did hers, and he quivered with anticipation as the combination of her posture and his nose told him something very important. Namely that she was a bitch in heat.

Hot damn.

Chuck. What was Chuck up to? Rommel knew that irritating human well enough to know that he, Rommel, could get involved in something infinitely pleasurable, only to be interrupted by some sort of trouble that Chuck had gotten himself into. Whatever Chuck was doing at the moment, was it safe? Was he relaxing in bed, or was he out above ground, getting involved in some new insanity that would compel Rommel to run off, trying to find him and save him from getting his fool human head shot off.

And Rommel was going to be damned if he was interrupted in the middle of this.

He sent out a cautious feeler to *the man,* trying to get a sense of him, and sure enough, there it was. Was he in danger? Was he in pain? Was he . . .

Rommel paused, tilting his head slightly. The bitch in heat growled impatiently, anxious to go one-on-one with this big hunk of dog, but Rommel would not be interrupted.

His cautious mental feeler told him that Chuck was up to something, and whatever it was, it wasn't dangerous. But—

At that moment the female came at him, and Rommel responded without hesitation and with uninhibited joy. Not for him were the moral complexities of should-he/shouldn't-he, does-she/doesn't-she. She was here, she was willing, she was his, and he was immediately all over her.

And he forgot to shut off the mental feeler to Chuck.

Connie came toward him, and Chuck caught her by the wrists.

"Connie," he said softly, trying not to be overwhelmed by the scent of her. "You have to understand. I really, truly, have strong feelings about how important—"

He stopped talking suddenly, in puzzlement, tilting his head slightly. He felt Rommel brushing against his mind, the most casual contact, like a moth flitting . . .

Connie began to nibble at the bottom of his neck. Her small but firm breasts were brushing against his bare chest.

He pushed her away, not angrily, but firmly. "Connie," he said, his heart pounding. "I don't . . ."

The room suddenly seemed to tilt sideways.

Chuck gasped in such a way that Connie drew back slightly, surprised. "Are you okay? What's wrong? Are you having a heart attack or something?"

Chuck's head snapped around, bizarre images flooding his mind. He started to pant heavily, and the room suddenly seemed alive with all sorts of scents. He was abruptly aware of the sweat under his arms that, for some reason, excited him. Her voice sounded sweet although the words were losing their meaning. He said something equally meaning-less in return—he thought it was words of endearment choked with passion, but he wasn't sure. He wasn't sure of anything except that suddenly there was nothing in the world but the two of them and the heat between them. He could smell that she wanted him, that she was hot for him. And he for her—my God, what was he waiting for?

He growled low in his throat and Connie stared at him. His mouth was hanging open, his breath coming in a staccato series of gasps, his tongue hanging partway out.

"Are you sure you're okay?" she asked.

He leaped at her.

* * *

Twin howls, from two different rooms, cut through the still air of the corridors underneath Wonderworld.

Chuck scratched at the back of his neck slowly. His arm stretched out automatically to find an empty space next to him, and for a moment he wasn't certain why he was disappointed to find it so.

Then he remembered, or did so partially. Memory came back to him in scattered fragments, random images filtered mostly through tactile sensations.

Perspiration. He remembered a lot of that. And . . . he frowned . . . lots of odd positions. And . . . barking . . .

"Oh, my God," he moaned, putting his face in his hands. "Oh, my dear God."

He lifted his head and looked around, and then came to a surprising realization.

He wasn't on the bed. He was on the floor. He looked up and saw the canopy hanging at an odd angle, because part of the right headpost had been broken. There was a rip through the top of the canopy, and a hole in the fitted sheet of the mattress as well.

He stood slowly, looking down to see that he was naked. His legs were unsteady, and the sheet was wrapped around them in twisted knots.

The pillows were gone. He found those in the bathtub, along with some more shredded sheet, and the shower curtain, which had been ripped down. Apparently the bathroom had seen its share of action. Back out in the sitting room he found the cushions of the couch scattered all over, the coffee table overturned . . . good Lord, hadn't any-place been safe from him?

And he couldn't remember a damned thing. The only thing that he knew for sure was that he had a dull ache in his crotch, the way that he had aches in any muscle that he hadn't exercised for a while and then had decided to give a really good workout. Also he had several bruises on his thighs and (from looking in the mirror) apparently several marks around his collarbone that used to be referred to—if he remembered correctly—as hickeys.

Barking . . .

Good Christ.

"Rommel!" he shouted. "Get *in* here!"

He didn't have to see the dog to know that his message got through. He felt it, and mere moments later the big German shepherd trotted into the room.

Rommel glanced around. *Busy night?*

"What did you do to me?" demanded Chuck.

Nothing.

"Rommel," said Chuck forcefully, "what were you up to last night?"

Humping. And you?

"Apparently the same thing."

Congratulations.

Chuck felt mortified. "I acted like an animal."

Good. There's hope for you.

"I didn't mean to! You got in my head and then you didn't get out!"

No need to thank me.

"I wasn't thanking you!" said Chuck, now wrapping a bathrobe around himself. "I'm ordering you never to do it again!"

Oh.

"Are we clear on this?"

Rommel stared at him. *Yes.*

"Good."

Rommel turned away and started to head toward the door. Just before he got to it, he glanced back at Chuck and said, *Admit it. It was great, and you're jealous.*

A smile played across Chuck's face for a moment, and he tried to get rid of it. "Maybe a little," he admitted.

Next time try thinking with your crotch a little more. You'll be happier. And he walked out.

"I'll keep that in mind," said Chuck.

Chuck stepped out of the shower and saw Connie standing there, dressed in a blue denim skirt and shirt.

He held the towel up in front of himself and said, "Look, Connie, about last night—"

"Wyatt wants to see you."

The no-nonsense tone of her voice brought him up short. "What's wrong?"

"He wants to see everybody. It's an emergency."

"What happened? What's going on—?"

"Wes is gone."

He blinked in surprise. "Wes? Wyatt's father?"

"Yes. He vanished sometime early this morning." She could not keep the worry out of her voice. "Wyatt thinks he may have been kidnaped."

10

WES GRIPPED THE steering wheel firmly and smiled to himself. The sun was glistening down upon him as the unending ribbon of roadway stretched out, beckoning him. It was another glorious day in southern California.

Moby sat next to him, patting him on the shoulder. "You're doing great, Wes," he said. "I never thought you had it in you."

"Ooooh," said Wes, "I'm full of surprises. You see, that's the advantage I have. I lived in a day where everything was new and everything was unexpected. Nowadays, everything's predictable. Everything's old hat. But not for me. Not for this Wonder."

"I'll say," said Moby, leaning back and planting his webbed feet on the dashboard. He mimed putting a cigarette to his beak, then blew a puff of genuine smoke that shaped itself into curlicues.

Wes looked at him disapprovingly. "Moby," he scolded, "I thought better of you than that."

"Sorry, Chief," said Moby contritely. He rolled down the window of the car and flicked out the nonexistent cigarette, then hurriedly rolled the window back up. "Gorgeous day."

"Absolutely," said Wes contentedly. All along the highway it was lined with green growing trees and bushes, stretching upward as high as if they could shake hands with passing clouds. The road sparkled, newly cleaned and glistening black with gleaming white lines painted down the middle. Not so much as a pothole to mar the vista or make the drive unpleasant. Although the car was moving at a good clip, small animated birds flew alongside it, keeping pace with it and cheerfully telling Wes to have a happy-appy-appy day.

And honks . . . the honks of animated geese as they fluttered overhead. And far, far in the distance, Los Angeles. Tall, gleaming spires, clean and pure and inviting. Los Angeles, where he'd grown up, where he'd created a company that had become a staple of the movie industry. Where he'd grown from a humble, ten man operation to a dependable entertainment concern that provided joy and laughter for millions of families throughout the world.

Wes Wonder was going home.

He didn't notice the car that came around and alongside him, or the driver who honked angrily and shouted, "Hey! Old man! You don't do thirty friggin' miles per hour in the high-speed lane! You got a goddamned limo, doesn't mean you own the friggin' road!" When the driver saw that Wes was paying him no heed at all, but instead seemed caught up in his own little world, he muttered a curse and flipped an obscene gesture at the old man.

The old man seemed to notice him for a moment, and waved cheerily. He mouthed something in greeting—what was it? Looked like—"Hi, Doofy." Doofy? The old man was calling him names of an old cartoon character?

The driver momentarily contemplated taking his gun out from under its secure place in his dash and blowing the old man's brains all over the inside of the nice limo. But then he thought better of it. He'd had a buddy pull the exact same offense last year, and after he'd been arrested he'd simply . . . disappeared. People did that far too frequently these days, and it was never a good idea to press one's luck. The driver shook his head, muttered to himself, and floored it to eighty miles per, still looking over his shoulder at the old man.

Unfortunately, because he wasn't paying attention, he hit one of the many potholes that studded the freeway. This one happened to be the size of Topeka—there had been a cone blocking it, but some kids had removed it an hour earlier. His left front tire hit it and then his left rear. He heard something shudder and snap and the car veered crazily. He cursed and fought to regain control of the vehicle. The onboard computer chip, sensing erratic driving and assuming that the driver was either drunk or incapacitated, tried to assume command of the steering, but it was too late. The car hurtled into the concrete divider with such force that the engine of the car was practically in the back seat. Unfortunately, of course, the driver was in the front. Now only the remains of the driver were in the front.

The car hurtled back across the highway, scattering cars in its path. It shot past the front of Wes's car, and Wes glanced at it without much interest, shaking his head sadly. All around him now were more honkings of more geese. He watched Doofy's car spin across the road and go up in flames. He drove past unharmed, of course, the luck of the old and the stupid guiding him as cars that had been moving at twice his speed were unable to get out of the way of the hurtling comet that one car had been transformed into.

"Poor Doofy Dog," said Wes. "Remember when we made that movie about driving safely, and how we had Doofy be the example of someone who goes crazy when they get behind a wheel?"

"Oh, yeah," said Moby. "I thought that was some of his best work."

"Yes, but I think he's taken it much too seriously," said Wes. "I mean, look at that."

Moby craned his neck to look out the back window at the flaming wreckage that was receding.

"The Doof always did throw himself into his work," admitted Moby.

"Yes. I know but . . . honestly," said Wes. "When we get back to the park, I'll have a talk with him. He's got to keep in mind that there's a difference between acting in movies and acting in real life." He shook his head sadly. "If there's anything more frightening in this world, it's some- one who can't distinguish between reality and fantasy."

11

CONNIE HAD REMAINED discreetly outside while Chuck hurriedly dressed. When he emerged he found not only Connie, but Rommel, both waiting for him just outside his quarters. Rommel and Connie seemed to be regarding each other with mutual suspicion, as if each was unsure about the other.

Chuck was tucking in his shirt, which was plastered onto his wet back since he hadn't taken the time to properly dry himself. He glanced from one to the other and said, "Problem here?"

"No. No problem," said Connie briskly, and she took him by the forearm. "Come on. I've never seen Wyatt this upset."

They walked quickly down the hallway, and Chuck was impressed by all the bustling about. He didn't have to be psychic to pick up on all the free-floating, massive anxiety that surrounded him. There was controlled hysteria all around him. He was almost choking on it.

He heard Wyatt's voice before he saw him. At first he thought that it was another one of Wyatt's "We-Want-You" presentations, but he realized a shocked moment later that the voice was unamplified. Wyatt was simply shouting at the top of his lungs, and it seemed very out of character for him. Wyatt Wonder was easily one of the most controlled individuals he'd ever met.

They entered a large conference room, to see Wyatt stalking it like a caged panther. His expression was ferral, his rage towering. His large fists were balled, and he was descending on one helpless individual, picked almost at random.

"Search the grounds again!" snarled Wyatt. "He's *got* to be here!"

"But, sir, I swear, he's not," said the man helplessly. He was dressed in one of those one-piece security uniforms, looking extremely ludicrous now with the smiling image of Moby Duck emblazoned across his back.

"You'll find him," said Wyatt furiously, his anger growing by the minute, "or so help me—" He drew back his hand, clearly ready to slam the head of the hapless guard. The guard, for his part, flinched, trying to ward off the blow.

The blow that never fell. Wyatt abruptly realized that he'd totally lost control of the arm. He could not make it descend. The guard stopped, puzzled at the seeming reprieve.

Wyatt struggled, but it was as if a vise clamp had snared the arm, refusing to let it budge. Then slowly, he realized, and turned toward Chuck. Chuck stood there, a few feet away, arms folded. Rommel was at his side and, upon seeing the big man's stare fall their way, growled a warning low in his throat.

"Everyone leave," snapped Wyatt. "Everyone except you two," he pointed at Chuck and Connie.

Rommel barked once, loudly and clearly.

"You three," Wyatt amended.

The other employees hurriedly cleared out. Wyatt's hand remained in that strange, uplifted position, but he seemed to be paying it no mind. It was as if he'd simply lost interest in that part of his body. As his men were leaving, he was still sharply issuing orders. "Spread out our search teams. Comb every part of the park—remember, my father knows this place like the back of his hand. And start squads combing the surrounding area. Check the motor pool. Make sure every vehicle is accounted for. Move. *Move.*"

Moments later the room was empty.

"Would you care to release my hand now," said Wyatt sharply.

The pressure on the hand was removed, and he flexed it momentarily. "You are not," he said slowly, with great and forced care, "ever to show me up in front of my other employees again. Is that understood." It was not a question.

"I understand that," said Chuck quietly. "Now there are two things you had best understand. First, I'm not your employee, so lumping me as 'other' is inappropriate. Second, no one is aware I 'showed you up' since, I presume, you've told no one else about my particular abilities. So when you didn't hit that poor, helpless individual, it was presumably chalked up to your forgiving nature."

They stared at each other for a moment, the air seeming to crackle between them. "You think you're hot shit," said Wyatt. "I've stepped on greater men than you to get to where I am today. Just remember that, Psi-Man."

"Get this straight, Wyatt. I don't think it. I *am* hot shit."

You tell him, Rommel said primly. *Want me to take a piece out of him?*

Chuck looked down at Rommel with a raised eyebrow. "Rommel wants to know if he should take a piece out of you."

Wyatt said nothing to this. Instead he walked back around the table until he reached the far end and then slowly sat down. With his great frame, it seemed to take forever. Once seated, he drummed on the table a moment, as if putting together his thoughts.

"He was like a god to me," said Wyatt slowly.

Connie and Chuck looked at each other. She shrugged.

"You have to understand," said Wyatt. "When I was growing up . . . my father was like a goddamned god. It was like—here was myself, and the rest of the world," and he waved his hand a couple inches above the table surface.

"And here was my father," and his other hand now stretched high above him. "I was in awe of him. Everybody knew him. Everybody. I lived in this closed world of show business where my father was loved and respected and, even to other people, like a god. You couldn't even say the word 'wonder' in any other context without it seeming to be my father. Wondowski. Did you know that? The family name was Wondowski. He changed his name to Wonder, and his father stopped speaking to him. My grandfather went to his deathbed and, even there, refused to so much as say good-bye to my father.

"Can you believe that? Can you believe anyone could be that cold?"

Chuck made no reply. None seemed required.

"Years later, though," he said slowly, "years later, people stopped caring. People started turning up their noses at 'family films.' Park attendance dropped. People stopped coming to see his movies. People started whispering, muttering that my father was no longer what he once was. Did you know how that made me feel?"

This time there was a longer pause, and Chuck knew that an answer was expected. "No one wants to feel that gods are mortals with feet of clay."

"A hard realization," said Wyatt Wonder. "And I swore, with every fiber of my being, that I would turn opinions around. Turn my father's business around. Do you believe that?"

"I'm not sure. I don't even believe I just heard someone say 'with every fiber of my being.' You've seen too many movies."

Wyatt smiled very thinly at that. "So I stepped in. My father . . . he was tired. Very, very tired. He had spent his life giving and giving and giving, and when no one wanted to take what he had to offer, he became an empty vacuum. And I took over . . ."

"With a vengeance," said Chuck.

Wyatt nodded slowly. "With a vengeance."

"Because you weren't just out to be a success. You were out to get everyone who had laughed at your father."

"Yes."

Now Wonder stood, looming, and he almost seemed as if his head might scrape against the ceiling. "As the years passed, and I became more and more powerful, and more and more important . . . as I became bigger and bigger . . . my father seemed to become smaller and smaller. I tried to involve him in what I was doing. I tried to get his approval of my expansion and reworking of the park. But nothing I did seemed to interest him. He would nod and smile and give tacit approval of my plans. Every time I'd buy out another movie company, acquire another property, he'd pat me on the back and say, 'Clever, son.' That's all he'd say. Not 'Tell me about how you did it' or 'What are your further plans' or even—I don't know— 'Good job.' Just 'Clever, son.' Like you'd pat a dog on the head for learning a new trick."

Rommel made a impolite *harrumph* sound.

If Wonder heard it, he gave no indication. "And he withdrew into himself. More and more. He started seeing Moby Duck everywhere."

"Well, so do I," said Chuck, not understanding. "He's on TV, movies, t-shirts, underwear—"

"No, I mean he really started to see him. The animated character, talking to him. And all the others. He totally lost whatever interest he had in the business side altogether, and he would spend his time just walking around the park, nodding and smiling and talking to characters who weren't there. And no one ever recognized him. Know that? Wes Wonder, walking around his own park, and people wouldn't recognize him. Know why? Because he'd lost the glow, you see. Wes Wonder never just entered a room. He *was* the room. He was bigger than the room. He would walk in, and just something about his aura would be like a star, pulling planets into orbit around him. He'd become the center of attention. He didn't need height, like me, or psychic powers, like you—or a bark like a cannon," he glanced at Rommel. "He just needed himself and his inner light. But like a fading star, the light stopped glowing from him, and everyone drifted away, falling out of their orbit."

"The only ones who didn't abandon him were the ones who came from his imagination," said Chuck.

"Yes. Exactly. And then, over a year ago while he was strolling around Wonderworld, he fell. When you're a young man, you just get back up. When you're an old man . . ."

"I know," said Chuck. "Brittle bones."

"Like kindling. Snaps"—and he snapped his fingers—"just like that. He wound up in a chair. We've both lived here on and off for many years, but when he was injured, I brought him down here to stay. He deserves to be near his park. And I made this my more-or-less permanent home—especially when our beloved president started getting more and more annoyed with me. Man has no sense of humor.

"But, Psi-Man . . . this morning we found my father's chair empty. I have my men searching the park, but that's really a lost cause. There's no way he's going to be on the grounds."

"He can walk," said Chuck.

Wonder snorted. "He hasn't left that chair in over a year."

"He snuck into my room and told me that he could walk."

"Really," said Wyatt, looking askance. "He snuck into my quarters last week and told me he could flap his arms and fly to the moon. Do you suggest we crack out telescopes to look for him?"

"I'm not suggesting anything."

"He was kidnaped," said Wonder forcefully. He started pacing. "Someone wants to get to me. I know it. Probably the president. He sent some members of his goon squad to try and strike at me at my weakest point."

"But it makes no sense," replied Chuck. "If someone was interested in getting you, and they were capable of breaking in, why wouldn't they just kill you once inside?"

Rommel, who had at this point become bored out of his skull, said impatiently, *You want to tell me what all this is about?*

"His father has vanished."

Wonder looked at Chuck in mild confusion, and then said, "Oh. You're talking to the dog again. Well, why not. This is certainly the place for it."

Old man?

"Yeah, Rommel. An old man. Now look, Wyatt—"

The one I saw sneaking out this morning?

Chuck stopped, his mouth hanging open, and he turned and looked at Rommel. "What did you say?"

"What did he say?" demanded Wonder.

Old man, heavy, light hair.

"Right. Right."

"What did he *say*?" Wonder said again, and then, "My God, I can't believe I'm pumping a dog for information."

He climbed into a large bin with clothing. I saw them wheel it away.

"A bin with clothing?" He turned to Wonder. "Do you—"

"A laundry cart?!" Wonder almost exploded. Chuck thought that Wonder might actually blow out the sides of the room. "He stowed away in a goddamn laundry cart?! How the hell did he do that?!"

"Maybe he can walk," said Chuck dryly.

At that moment one of Wonder's security guards came in, snapping off a salute. He was very young, and Chuck immediately assumed it was bad news. Probably none of the senior officers wanted to deliver it, and so they had assigned one of the newest recruits to do the deed.

"What is it?" demanded Wonder.

"Sir, one of—" His voice cracked, and was hoarse. Chuck was reminded of the old joke about seeing people in hell, standing in a pool of shit that was only up to their knees, and in comparison to other damned souls who were hip deep or even neck deep in shit, it wasn't so bad. And then Satan says, "Okay, break time's over. Everybody back to standing on your head." That's what this guard looked like right now—like somebody who would rather be doing handstands in shit than delivering the news he was about to deliver. "One of the limos is missing."

"Missing," said Wonder. If he was as amazed as he

sounded, he was doing a good job of hiding it. "Would you mind telling me how that's possible?"

"It wasn't in the main motor pool, sir. It was in the repair shop. They'd just finished it up the night before, and they hadn't returned it yet. And there's a separate entrance to the repair shop that doesn't require people to exit out the main gate . . ."

Wonder was ashen. He'd been the one who designed the underground. He had no one to blame but himself. "I see," he said, barely above a whisper. "Thank you."

The guard stood frozen in place, seemingly unable to believe that that was all there was to it. "Leave," said Wonder, and the guard did not need another invitation.

Wonder slowly sat down, shaking his head in amazement. "I can't believe I overlooked that," he said. "I can't believe I left that exit unguarded." He looked up and, for a moment, looked more vulnerable than Chuck had ever seen him. Even during his lengthy discussion of his father, Wyatt had still appeared every inch the invincible business mogul. Now, for just a moment, Chuck saw a confused individual—

Who promptly vanished. The mask reappeared, and Wonder composed himself completely. "We have to find him."

"We'll find him," said Chuck. "But we have to have some idea where to look."

"We'll find him, all right. At least we'll find the car. All the limos have built in locaters. As long as he's within the car, he'll be found. Come on."

He walked out quickly, followed by Chuck and Connie. And Chuck heard in his head, *Don't anyone thank me or anything.*

Moments later they'd entered a room filled with various high-tech equipment. Chuck looked around, impressed. Connie appeared vaguely uncomfortable, and Rommel just seemed bored.

Wonder, meantime, was standing over a technician, a young black man, who was already punching up images on a screen. Chuck came over and stood just behind them. "How do they know which limo to look for?"

"My people already got the frequency code from the records the moment they found it was gone," said Wonder. "They didn't need me to tell them that."

"How fortunate."

"There. Got it . . . shit," said the technician. "Hold on. I'm crosschecking something. Yeah, I was afraid of that. Look."

A small, glowing dot was moving across the screen, and the technician had just superimposed a map over it.

Connie had now put one of her small, delicate hands on Wonder's arm. "Wherever he is," she said softly, "at least it's not as bad as you thought it was."

"Could be worse than bad," said the technician, blowing a bubble from a wad of gum. "That's downtown L.A. he's heading into. Worst section of town. He goes in there, he'd better be heavily armed, or he ain't coming out again."

12

REUEL BEUTEL STEPPED off the plane at LAX and was immediately met, as he came down the stairway, by several men in dark suits similar to his. Beutel smiled and gave a quick inclination of his head as the agents surrounded him and matched his quick strides. "Bring me up to speed, boys," he said briskly.

"Something is going on at the park," said the largest one, a man whose jacket seemed tight on his large shoulders. His name, Beutel remembered, was Kendall. "Our people in there said the place has been bustling with more security men than usual. They're all looking for something."

"Looking for something," said Beutel, his mind racing. "Like what."

"Impossible to determine at the moment."

"Let's make it possible."

"We're in constant comlink with them. As soon as they find out, we'll find out."

Chuck stood in the carport as high-speed vehicles were being rolled up. Limos weren't the only thing at Wyatt Wonder's disposal. Chuck was impressed to see the latest hardware rolling his way—the computer-aided RAC 3000,

Ultraflame Model. More horsepower than the chariot race in *Ben-Hur,* capable of going zero to sixty in something like minus 2 seconds. Just for kicks he'd once priced out one of the things. The monthly payments alone ran more than he made in a decade.

Yet there it was, and there were three more rolling up behind it. It was gleaming red. He'd always wanted a red car. Red cars were the symbols of lunatics. You were allowed to drive insanely when you owned a car that was flaming red. It was almost expected of you.

Rommel sniffed at the tires and regarded the car suspiciously. He was accustomed to riding in the backs of pickup trucks or whatever piece of garbage that Chuck was able to beg, borrow, or steal. But this thing—this thing looked like a guided missile on wheels.

"Wow" was all he could think to say.

Wonder ran up and rapped on the hood. "Computer's already preprogrammed, Chuck. You're leading the team."

"*I'm* leading the team?" said Chuck incredulously. "No. I don't want to be the leader."

Wonder placed hands on both of Chuck's shoulders. "Grow up, Psi-Man. You have power. You're a special individual. That carries a price with it . . . with great power comes great responsibility."

"Where did you hear that?"

"Got it out of a comic book. Liked it so much I bought the whole company. Chuck—I trust you with this. I trust you with my father's life."

"If you care so much about him, why don't you come along?"

Wonder stared at him for a moment. "Because I have you. And because I know that since you're aware that my father is in trouble, you can't just stand aside and not do anything about it. Well"—and he gestured—"here it is. Here's your means of doing something about it," and he patted the car. "When you get back with my father, you can keep it."

"Bribe?"

"Gesture of esteem."

Chuck stared at him. "I'll bring him back. And then I'm leaving."

Connie had been standing there, looking from one to the other, and now her eyes widened. "Leaving?"

Rommel looked up. *Leaving?*

"This place isn't for me," he said almost sadly. "I'm looking for something that you wouldn't quite understand. I don't even know if I fully understand it."

I certainly don't, Rommel informed him.

And Connie said suddenly, "When you leave . . . I want to come too."

Wonder turned and looked at her, his eyes narrowing. "Connie," he said slowly, "I don't think that would be wise, do you?"

She looked down, then back up at him, her eyes determined. "Maybe not. But I want to."

"It's not a good idea," said Chuck, "but we'll discuss it later. Come on, Rommel." He opened the door and gestured. Rommel sat there a moment, regarding him suspiciously.

You sure about this?

"I'm sure. Now come on."

Rommel hopped forward and settled himself into the driver's seat. He leaned his paws on the steering wheel and looked expectantly at Chuck.

"No," said Chuck firmly.

Rommel moped a moment and then insinuated his huge body into the passenger seat. Chuck climbed in and slammed the door behind him. The cars that were lined up behind him were also quickly manned.

Wonder would have liked to send an army, but he didn't think it wise. He knew, or at least suspected, that certain government forces watched the comings and goings out of Wonderworld with careful attention. If a massive convoy were mounted, it would certainly attract notice, and that was the last thing that Wonder wanted to do. He tossed off a salute.

Chuck saw it and saluted back.

Why did you do that?

"Gesture of respect."

But you don't respect him.

"How do you know?"

Because when you think about him, you smell bad.

"Great," muttered Chuck. "Just great. I can't think of anything worse than a talking dog."

"Good day, Mr. Simon," said the car in a polite female tone.

Chuck's eyes widened. He now saw the speaker situated in the middle of the steering wheel. "Uh . . . hello. Nice day."

"Sixty-two degrees Fahrenheit," said the car. "Thirty percent chance of precipitation. Skies overcast. Air quality is poor. If you have a bronchial condition, you are recommended to stay indoors."

"Great. Just great."

The car's talking.

"I know the car's talking, Rommel."

Dumbest thing I ever heard. Talking car.

Chuck glanced at Rommel, a fairly obvious remark on his lips, but he opted instead to let it pass.

"You got a name, car?"

"I am the RAC 3000."

"What does RAC stand for?" he asked.

"Really Awesome Car."

"Oh." He shrugged. Obviously a name developed by people in marketing. "Okay. Let's go."

"Destination?"

He paused. "Have you got a computer lock on the signal from the limo we want to find?"

"Yes, Mr. Simon. It's already been programmed in."

"Okay. Let's go."

"Shall I drive or would you prefer to drive?"

Why aren't we moving?

"It wants to know if I should let it drive."

You let it drive, I'm getting out.

"I think I'll drive," Chuck informed the car. It wasn't a difficult decision—Rommel's concerns mirrored Chuck's

own. Hell, he'd never even been comfortable with cruise
control.

"Manual control confirmed." On a blank console panel
to his right, a schematic of the area appeared. One particular
road glowed more brightly than the others. "Most efficient
route to destination now indicated on map panel."

"Thank you," said Chuck.

You're thanking the car.

"Yes, I know, Rommel. It was helpful."

It's not alive.

"How do you know?" said Chuck crisply as he reached
down for the key . . . and didn't find it. Instead there was
a small, thumb-sized pad next to the steering column.
"Where's the key?"

"Place your thumb against the starter pad," the car said.

Chuck did so. The car roared to life.

"Your individual print has now been keyed into the
onboard security system," the car told him. "No one else is
authorized to start this RAC 3000 unit."

"Well . . . good," said Chuck. This was too much. In
his hometown there had been none of this high-tech stuff.
Life had changed very little in LeQuier over the years.
Indeed, residents had been almost pathologically resistant to
the notion. So being confronted now by this state-of-the-art
stuff—Animagic ducks and talking cars—it was like taking
a big step off a pier and falling into fantasy land.

He said as much to Rommel.

Right, agreed Rommel. *So says the fugitive aikido master
telekinetic Quaker to the telepathic dog.*

"Good point," admitted Chuck.

He put his foot to the gas (at least that was where it was
supposed to be) and the car roared forward. Chuck was
almost intimidated by it, for he sensed the vehicle's pure
power. Still, in the back of his mind, he knew he needn't be
worried. The thing probably had some sort of internal
backup systems that prevented any major mishaps, even
with a mere mortal driving.

The other cars fell into line behind him, and they barreled

out of Wonderworld. Chuck wondered if the other drivers were having chats with their cars as well.

"You are now proceeding southwest toward Los Angeles at a speed of fifty-seven miles per hour," the car said.

"Thanks, Rac," Chuck said.

"Query, Mr. Simon—why are you addressing me with my model name?"

"Well, I have to call you something," said Chuck.

This name business again? Rommel grunted. Chuck had tried to make his life miserable by going on ad nauseam about the importance of names and similar nonsense. He'd saddled him with this "Rommel" business through a chain of typically human logic that made as much sense to Rommel as did most other things typically human. Now he was inflicting it on the car. At least the car wasn't alive.

"Yes, the name business again," Chuck told Rommel testily

I'm hungry.

"Later."

I'm still hungry.

"I mean it, Rommel, knock it off," said Chuck as he turned onto the entrance for the highway. "Remember, I'm your master."

Rommel turned a pitying gaze on him. *You're not serious.*

Chuck didn't deign to answer that one.

"Music, Mr. Simon?" asked Rac. "I have a catalogue of over three thousand selections."

Chuck smiled. "Okay. Uhm . . . got any Seduction of the Innocent? It's rock music."

Immediately the strains of something that sounded classical filled the interior of the car. "That's not rock," said Chuck in confusion.

"Yes it is, sir. Rachmaninoff, as you requested."

Rommel started to sing along with it, his howling combining with the music to produce a cacophonous mess. "Knock it off!" shouted Chuck.

It helps me forget how hungry I am.

Chuck sighed. This had the makings of a very long trip.

* * *

Connie had a fondness for Pioneerland. In a world that was endlessly confusing and complicated, there was a pure straightforwardness about it. Calm. Very calm indeed, despite the abundance of cowboys, Indians, and settler types ranging around. As with all the areas of Wonderworld, it was a fascinating mix of live action and Animagic, carefully combined to the point where even she wasn't always clear on which was what.

Curiously enough, the Haunted House had been placed in Pioneerland, probably because of the early American look of the structure. Connie strolled along the waiting line, glancing at the various people waiting with anticipation to get their turn, for the Haunted House was truly legendary. It had a reputation for being an odd combo of scary, and yet unthreatening, due to the dazzling special effects nature of the ride.

Someone tapped Connie on the shoulder. She turned and saw a man and a woman, both in their forties and, to Connie's surprise, clearly both blind. Their clouded eyes seemed to glisten at her, and they both had small radar sets attached to their ears. Replacing inefficient canes long ago, radar sets emitted batlike emissions that bounced back and enabled blind people, after a week or so of practice, to judge distances and objects in front of them to within millimeters.

"Excuse me," said the man. "Is this the line for the Haunted House?"

She nodded and then realized and said, "Yes, it is."

"Excellent. Come on, June," and he took the woman's arm, in order to lead them to the end of the line.

But Connie took them by the arms and said, "No, wait. It's okay. Come on . . . I work here."

"We don't want any pity or special favors," said the woman who had been called June. "Just because we're blind doesn't entitle us to anything special."

Connie smiled dazzlingly, knowing it was wasted, but unable to help herself. "It's park policy to give special consideration to special guests."

"Nice euphemism," said the man. He was half smiling.

"At any rate, it is park policy, and I just can't go against policy, now, can I?"

"You work here?" said June. "Ward, she works here."

"Can't have her getting in trouble on account of us," replied Ward.

Taking each one of them by one arm, she guided them to the front of the line and into the mansion. The people she passed on line, some of whom had been there for close to an hour, nevertheless nodded and smiled as she went past with them. Out in the "real" world, people were shot for jumping forward in line. But somehow in Wonderworld, everything was peaceful and serene. Moving blind people to the front? Go right ahead. Everything is wonderful in Wonderworld.

She walked them past the ride operators, who naturally recognized Connie immediately. Everyone throughout Wonderworld knew Connie on sight. She had, after all, been with Wyatt Wonder for as long as any could remember.

One saw the Haunted House by riding in small, individual riding cars that were shaped like an egg and glided noiselessly along tracks. On either side various holograms and Animagics hurled themselves at you, although of course never crossing over the "ghostly barrier" to actually touch you. Accompanied by recorded screams and spooky music, and of course the patented preternatural darkness, it was all good, clean, weird fun.

The cars accommodated three riders at the most, and as Connie helped them in, Ward said, "I hate to ask this of you . . . but would you mind terribly riding along and telling us what's around us? The music and sound effects are wonderful, but it would be nice to—"

"Now, Ward," June scolded him, in such a way that Connie knew they must have been married for quite some time. "The young lady certainly has more important things to do."

"No, no, it's quite all right." Connie smiled. "I haven't been through the Haunted House in ages anyway." She climbed in between them and the car started on its route as, ten feet behind them, another car rolled up to take on new passengers.

"First time here?" she asked.

"Oh, yes," said Ward. "We saved up money for years to finally come here from Wichita. It's everything we hoped it would be."

"More," confirmed June.

The car began its twisting and turning path, and Connie said, "Now over there is—"

"Listen carefully," said Ward. Suddenly his voice had changed. It was stern and sharp, and even menacing. "Security guards are running all over the place like headless chickens. Tell us what's going on."

"What?" She looked at him in confusion, and then at June. June's expression mirrored Ward's.

"What's going on? Bring us up to speed, right now, Miss Lopez, and we won't hurt you." June's voice cut like ice.

"I don't understand." Despite the fact that it was strictly against rules, Connie tried to haul herself out of the ride and jump out. But the blind couple pulled her back down again, hard.

"How—how did you know my name?" she stammered out.

"We know who you are, Miss Lopez. That's all you need to know," said Ward. "That, and that unless you tell us immediately what's going on, we'll kill you."

"You're . . ." She looked frantically from one to the other. She opened her mouth, about to scream.

"Scream, we slit your throat right now," warned June.

The scream caught in her throat and she choked out, "You're not b-blind."

"Reflective contacts, specially designed," said Ward. "Very effective. Your little retina scanners don't penetrate them, but we still have eighty percent sight."

"Stop boasting, dammit," said June harshly. "Now, Miss Lopez—tell us why Wonderworld's on red alert. Tell us right now, or tell no one anything else, ever again."

"But . . ."

The woman held up her long fingernails. Connie looked at them. Whatever they were, they weren't fingernails. The edges looked razor-sharp.

"Three seconds, and then I'll carve out your eyeballs, and you'll be like us . . . except we can take the lenses out at the end of the day."

"Wes Wonder's gone," said Connie quickly. "They'd combed the park for him, but now they think he escaped."

Ward and June looked at each other in the darkness. Around them ghosts howled, and a specter reached for them, stopping short by inches. They paid it no mind. "Escaped," said Ward.

"Perfect. And Simon?"

Connie said nothing.

June's finger sliced across Connie's forearm, and she shrieked.

"Didn't even cut you," said June, fingering the edge of a sliced piece of fabric. "Next time I will. I can cut both your wrists. You'll bleed to death in the ride and you'll permanently haunt this place."

"Simon went in search of him," said Connie, terrified. "They think he's heading toward downtown L.A."

"The old man won't last five minutes," said Ward.

"I know," June agreed. She looked at Connie. "Tell me everything else."

Connie told her as much as she knew, the words tumbling one over the other. She couldn't recall ever having been this terrified in her entire life, and wondered if she was going to live to be this terrified ever again.

She looked up and saw light in front of her. The ride was ending. She couldn't remember it ever taking this short of a time before and yet, at the same time, it seemed an eternity.

Suddenly she felt a pressure against her arm, then a quick sting. She looked down in horror.

June was withdrawing a hypodermic.

"You—you . . ." she stammered.

"It will be quick," said June dispassionately.

Next to her, Ward said in annoyance, "Now was that really necessary?"

"Yes. You don't want them to be alerted that we know," June told him, "It'll look like she died of a heart attack. Could buy us a few hours, which is what we'll need."

The woman had killed her. She was talking as if Connie weren't even here, and she sobbed.

"Quick," said June. "Quick and clean. The best I could do."

"Sometimes," said Ward grumpily, "I really hate this job."

Connie slumped forward and blacked out.

13

THEY HAD MADE extraordinary time, for other cars had simply gotten the hell out of the way as the small convoy of RAC 3000 Flamebirds shot down the highway. They'd done everything short of leave a sonic boom behind them.

Yet Chuck was gnawed by the idea that no matter how fast they were going, it might still not be fast enough.

He glanced at the chronometer on the dashboard. It told him that it was a little after twelve noon. Of course, it was impossible to tell that from the sky, what with the sun seemingly hidden forever behind a perpetual gray haze.

"Twenty-two minutes until vehicle contact," the car told him in that pleasant voice of hers. It was so sweet-sounding that it almost helped him forgive the eighteenth-century waltz that was now oozing sweetly out of the speakers.

"Are you sure you can't play some rock and roll?" he pleaded. "Something snappy?"

Rac switched to "The Flight of the Bumblebee." "It's better for you," she told him firmly.

"Great." He glanced at Rommel. Rommel had climbed into the back seat and was stretched out as much as his great bulk would allow him. His eyes were closed and his chest rising and falling steadily. "Just great."

Then he glanced at the blip that was representing his goal and suddenly realized something. "He's stopped moving," Chuck said.

"That is correct."

"Could he be out of gas or something? Broken down?"

"Records show that the vehicle had just had maintenance done on it. Immediate breakdown is unlikely. It was fully gassed at the time of departure, and the trip from Wonderworld to downtown L.A. would not exhaust the gas supply."

"Okay," said Chuck slowly. "Then . . . why did he stop?"

Wes slammed the door behind him, and then he heard an outraged *squawk*. He turned in time to realize, to his mortification, that he had accidentally caught Moby's webbed foot in the door. Moby was yanking on it with all his strength, grunting and giving Wes a nasty look.

"I'm so sorry, Moby," said Wes. "Let me help you . . ."

Moby pulled so hard that his leg elongated to a ludicrous length, and then suddenly pulled free. Moby sailed, end over end, to impact against the wall of the building and flatten like a pancake. Wes hurried over and slowly peeled the flattened fowl off the wall. He looked at Moby sadly, and then made a brisk snapping motion with his wrists. Moby, through the magic of animation, promptly snapped back into his normal shape and dimensions. He flexed his arms and shook his head. "You sure make my life exciting, pal."

"Sorry, Moby," said Wes again sincerely. "It was an accident."

"Yeah, well, be careful next time." He gestured toward the building they were standing in front of. It was three stories tall, burned out as were many of the buildings in the area they'd come to, with graffiti all over it and boards upon the walls.

Except that wasn't what Wes saw.

"Don't you remember, Moby?" said Wes. "This is where you were born. This is your home. Look. Look, up there is my old office," and he pointed to a window on the upper right. As were all the other windows, it was boarded over. "Look at the way the sun glints off the glass—it always did in those days, Moby. Decades ago, when I was young. When we were all young. I was a kid, you were a hatchling. We grew up together. Except now they're gone," he said a bit wistfully. "Nate. Jack, Robbie, and Casey. Gone, all gone. All the guys who started with me.

"But"—and he slapped his belly firmly—"I shouldn't be sad. I got my health. And I got my building. That's why we've come back here, Moby. This was the Wonder Academy—that's what we called it. We were the whiz kids. We made magic happen here, my good duck. And we will again. It's sitting here, not a brick different from what it was years ago."

Moby eyed it cautiously. "I thought you abandoned it years ago, Wes. When the animation setup was moved to the big building out in the hills."

"Oh, that place," and Wes made a dismissive gesture. "Sure, sure, I suppose so. But that's really Wyatt's operation now. Not mine. He thinks I'm an old man, Moby." He tapped himself on the chest. "Me. He thinks I can't do it anymore. Well, he's wrong."

"So what do you care what he thinks?" demanded Moby.

Wes thought a moment and then frowned. "I don't know. But I do. And I'm going to show him that this 'old man' still has what it takes. I'm setting up shop here again, Moby. I'm going to make my own animated films."

"How? All by yourself?" he asked skeptically.

"Oh, they'll come. When they hear about the studio opening up again here, they'll come. All the animators whose parents were kids back when I first started, they'll come to me, begging for the chance to work with Wes Wonder." He thumped his fist into his palm. "I'm going to show them. I'll show them all."

"Wes . . . have you taken a look at this place? I mean, really taken a look?"

Wes Wonder shrugged his shoulders. "Oh, it's a little

dusty, I'll admit. Could use a coat of paint here and there. A few touch-ups. But the structure is sound."

He thudded his fist against the wall. A piece of brick crashed to the ground three feet from him. He didn't notice it.

"That's what's important, Moby," he said firmly, continuing obliviously. "If the structure is there, then something can be built. That's the way it is in life, and that's the way in imitations of life. Come on."

He headed for the door, a solid, rusting hunk of iron that hung crazily on its hinges. "Let's take a look around inside," said Wes.

"You think it's wise?" Moby asked.

"Don't be a chicken, duck," Wes remonstrated him. He pulled on the door that, at first, resisted his meager strength. But then slowly it moved on its rusted hinges and swung open.

"After you," said Moby with questionable graciousness. Wes inclined his head and walked in.

He stopped just inside and looked around, smiling. "Yes," he said. "Yes, it's all just as I remember it."

Once again Moby was doubtful. "You remember working in a dump, do you, Wes?"

"What's the matter with you, Moby?" Wonder frankly couldn't understand it. "You're usually much more supportive than this."

"Maybe," Moby said, "maybe this time it's getting tough for even me to back you on this."

"Moby," said Wes sharply, "either we're in this together or you can stay behind right here and now. No more arguing."

"Hey, I'm with you, Wes. You know that," said Moby Duck softly.

"All right then," replied Wes. "Now up here is where the bullpen was. None of this claustrophobic cubical stuff."

He started up the rickety stairs, narrowly missing large holes that were a result of weakened and rotting boards. "A big, open area so that the artists can exchange ideas, talk back and forth. Spontaneity is what causes the best ideas, and the best cartoons. Always remember that, Moby."

"I'll remember it, Wes. I'll remember everything you say."

"Good." He stopped, turned, and patted the duck on his back. "That's good to hear."

Wes made it up to the second floor and stopped.

There, seated, in the middle of his bull pen, were about a half a dozen sullen youths. The air hung heavy with the stench of human odor and decay. Their clothes were in tatters, their hair filthy and lice-ridden. A rat was crawling over the legs of one of them, and barely received more than a passing glance.

Their eyes were widened and red, their tongues lolling slightly out. Whatever individuality they may have had had slowly disappeared over the course of long months of continued Snap ingesting, to blend gradually into a uniform look of hopeless semihumanity.

But not so hopeless that they couldn't detect prey when it was near.

They looked up at Wes slowly. They were between hits, just at the tail end of the previous high and contemplating what they would do, where they would go, whom they would kill, in order to achieve their next one.

Wes stood in the doorway, looking at them in amazement.

"Moby," he told the duck to his right. "Why are Pistol Pete and Wall-Eyed Pike and Doofy . . . why are they all lying around here in the middle of the floor? Don't they know there's work to be done?"

The Snappers stared at him, then at one another in silent communion and agreement. Then they rose up, slowly, like specters.

"I don't like the looks of this, Wes," said Moby nervously.

"Of course you don't, Moby. This isn't the way that 'toons should be conducting themselves." He clapped his hands briskly. "Come on, boys. I want us all to get together for a think session."

The Snappers surrounded him, silently, as if trying to figure out what reason his existence might have before they snuffed him out and took whatever he had on him, for the purpose of barter. One of them, close to Wes, drew back his lips to display several rotting teeth, accompanied by a low, animalistic growl.

"Humphrey Hippo, how you've let yourself go," said Wes, and he patted the Snapper on the cheek.

As one, they leaped on him, galvanized into life by a mutual mission of destruction.

Moby screamed as Wes was borne down to the floor. "You can't do this! Stop! Stop!"

"Moby, help me!" howled Wes. "They've gone crazy! *Help!*"

Moby ducked out. He went quackers. Within seconds he'd gone from a ninety-pound weakling to 250 pounds of pure feathered fury. With a roar like an express train, Moby Duck leaped to the rescue.

"The vehicle is now proceeding west," the car informed Chuck.

Chuck grunted in annoyance. Even with the glowing indicator in front of him, he was still having trouble navigating his way through the streets of downtown L.A. And now it seemed Wonder was on the move again.

"Shall I overtake?" inquired Rac politely.

Chuck thought quickly. Doing this manually, it could take forever. "All right," he said. "You drive."

Rommel picked his head up. *What are you doing?*

"I'm letting the car drive."

Let me out.

"Don't be a baby."

Even if Chuck had wanted to, he couldn't have, because at that moment the car suddenly hurtled forward. Chuck had been navigating the streets carefully at forty miles per hour. Rac immediately kicked it up to sixty, maneuvering the streets as easily as if they'd been on the highway. And the speed climbed.

The cars behind Chuck automatically increased their

speed to keep up. To Chuck's surprise, and Rommel's chagrin, a siren began to wail, and Chuck thought that a cop was following them until he realized that they were the source of the siren. Rommel tried to put his paws over his ears and was only partly successful.

Rac barreled through stoplights as what few other cars there were on the road screeched to a halt or swerved to get out of the way. Pedestrians crossing the street leaped aside to give the car a wide berth.

"Be careful!" shouted Chuck. "Don't hurt anyone!"

"I am programmed not to bring harm to any other vehicle or pedestrian," said Rac primly, and then added, "unless otherwise instructed."

"Well I'm not otherwise instructing you," said Chuck. "Just watch it!"

"Yes, Mr. Simon."

The car screeched around another corner and sped forward. Chuck looked down at the tracker and saw, to his surprise, that they had almost overtaken it. He looked out the windshield and, sure enough, there was the limo.

The limo was acting even more insanely than Rac was. The big car was swerving from side to side, as if drunk. Wonder was apparently totally heedless of those around him.

"He's gone completely nuts," said Chuck. "Rac, overtake him, now."

The car sped up, and Rommel yowled, *I really hate this!*

"Shut up, Rommel!"

I could be back at the park, humping and eating, but no—

"I'm warning you, Rommel! Not another word!"

Nonchalantly, as if she were utterly unoccupied in a high-speed car chase, Rac inquired, "Mr. Simon, to whom are you speaking?"

"The dog."

"Permit me to observe, sir" (*screech, wumpf* went the car) "that talking to a dog in that fashion is patently absurd," the car told him.

Once again Chuck considered the obvious response, but

again didn't make it. Instead he clutched firmly onto the dashboard and tried not to vomit.

Rac drew alongside the speeding limo, and Chuck glanced to his left. The windows were rolled down.

It was not Wes Wonder at the wheel.

Instead it was some punks. Red jackets. Christ, the ones from the other day. Didn't they have anything better to do than have an obsession with cars?

The driver looked to his right, saw the car that was pursuing him, and his eyes widened in recognition when he saw Chuck. Chuck gestured firmly and said, "Pull over!"

The punk in the passenger seat brought a gun up, aimed, and fired.

The shot hit the window right in front of Chuck's face, and he flinched in surprise. A small pockmark was raised on the glass, but that was all. Bulletproof.

"They're shooting. How rude," observed Rac. "And I was just cleaned."

The limo suddenly swerved to cut them off. Rac immediately swung sharply off to the right to avoid impact. She hit the curb, sending two passing bums running for their lives. She skidded up onto the sidewalk and sped down it, her right front fender scraping the building, her left almost clipping a fire hydrant. She swung back out onto the street in the next intersection, and there was the screeching of tires from behind as the cars following them almost plowed into her.

The limo had kept on going, and Rac kicked back into gear. Chuck looked down and saw the gas pedal hit the floor by itself. The car roared forward with the sorts of sounds Chuck thought only existed during chase scenes in movies.

"I think it's pissed," he told Rommel.

I know I am, replied the dog.

The car pulled alongside once again. This time Chuck was ready. The moment he saw the gun brought to bear by the passenger punk, he grabbed it with his mind and yanked. The gun hurled from the car and fell onto the street, clattering away. The punk looked behind him, amazed, then looked at Chuck who was once again warning them to pull over. The punk quickly rolled up the window and the limo started to accelerate.

"Enough of this chasing stuff," said Chuck, and he reached out with his mind. He probed the hood of the limo, found the latch, and unlocked it. The hood flew up in the faces of the drivers, completely obstructing their view. The limo veered crazily, and Rac sped up and passed the limo. Chuck glanced over his shoulder, studied the engine for a moment, and then mentally yanked out wires. He wasn't much for how motors worked, but he correctly reasoned that the more things that are ripped out of where they should be, the less chance a car has of operating.

The engine cut out and the steering seized up. Totally out of control, the car sailed into the side of an abandoned building, crashing into it with a hideous crunching of metal.

Rac swung around, and the other cars went past and also swerved around to follow. Rac rolled forward about fifty yards and then came to a halt. Chuck shoved the door open, then glanced behind him.

"Come on!" Chuck shouted to Rommel.

Come on yourself. I don't feel well. My head still hurts from the siren.

"That's what a little easy living does to you," said Chuck in annoyance as he jumped out of the car.

The punk in the passenger seat was trying to shove the limo door open, but the impact had jammed it shut. He saw Chuck coming and reached around to try to find something to shoot with. When nothing was forthcoming, the punk climbed out the window, turned, and started to run as fast as he could.

Chuck's mind reached out and yanked the punk's legs out from under him. He went down in a swirl of his red jacket.

Scrambling out from the other side now came the driver, and his eyes flickered in recognition. "Yeah, I thought it was you. What the hell you want from me, man?"

The other security guards had come running up, and they were holding the passenger facedown on the ground. The driver had slid over the crumpled hood and stood facing

Chuck, looking as tough as he could. Indeed, Chuck sensed no fear from him.

"You got a problem, man?" said the punk again.

"Where's the driver?" said Chuck tersely.

"You're looking at him."

"The old man who was driving this car."

"This is my car. Graduation present." The punk was sneering, and Chuck longed to wipe it off him. But what was he supposed to do? Pound the kid into submission? That wasn't Chuck's way. Besides, this was one tough bastard. Physical abuse would only toughen him up further, and accomplish nothing in any event.

He didn't like to use his psi powers openly, but now he had no choice. Time was flying past, and Wes Wonder might even now be lying in an alleyway somewhere with blood pouring out of him.

The next thing the punk knew he was airborne.

His arms and legs pinwheeled frantically as the ground deserted him, or more correctly, he deserted the ground. He screamed and howled, and Chuck was utterly unmoved by his pleas. The punk sailed ten feet straight up and then hung there.

If the security men were at all surprised, they didn't show it. Chuck was pleased about that.

"What are you doing?!" shrieked the punk.

"What's your name, son?" asked Chuck in his best gym-teacher voice.

"Viper!"

Viper suddenly went another ten feet in the air and when he stopped it was not with a gentle motion.

"Try again," said Chuck softly.

"Don! Don! My name is Don!" howled Viper.

"All right, Donny," he deliberately added a bit of accent to the diminutive. "You're currently about, oh, twenty feet in the air? If you don't answer my question, you'll be thirty feet in the air. Then forty and so on."

"What ARE you?!"

Now assuming his nastiest, most evil tone, Chuck said, "I'm Psi-Man. And the problem is, I don't know just how powerful I am. I might send you up too high for me to support you, and then you'll fall and be rather crushed. Or, for all I know, I'm powerful enough to send you so high you'll be clipped by a passing airplane. Neither one sounds like a great deal of fun, does it, *Don*ny."

"Fuck you!" yelled Viper. "I'm not telling you any—" and suddenly he was flung upward even higher. Then he stopped so abruptly he thought his spine was going to rip out his back; his internal organs were going to leak out his ears and nose. Far below him stood the men, looking up, and now the one who'd called himself Psi-Man was shouting as loudly as he could.

"Either way I win, *Don*ny. You see, if you refuse to cooperate and I get bored or whatever, I let you go and we've got one less punk to deal with. And the demonstration, I'm sure, will convince your friend here."

Viper started to whimper.

"Problems, *Don*ny?"

"We didn't see a driver," and he could barely get his voice above a terrified whisper.

Consequently, Chuck didn't hear what he said. "Come again?"

"We didn't see a driver!" howled Viper, managing to get air into his lungs. He thought sure he was going to black out. "The car was parked! I swear! We were just stealing it! We didn't do anything to anybody! I swear to God! Please don't kill me. Please, please, man," and he started to sob piteously.

He descended, with horrifying speed. The ground whirled up toward him and he knew that absolutely, right now, this instant, he was going to die, and cripes, what a stupid way to die, for some stupid limo that got wrecked and he was taking the fall for offing someone that he'd never even seen . . .

He slowed down. Then sped up, slowed down, in a herky-jerky motion that nearly made him ill. And suddenly the ground was right under his feet.

Chuck took him by the shirtfront and snarled into his face—"Where?"

* * *

"Spread out," ordered Chuck.

They had gone to the area where Viper, né Donny, had stated he'd gotten the car. He couldn't remember exactly in front of which building it was situated, and Chuck wasn't able to get any specific psychic reading. A feeling such as the one he had garnered from the terrified boy, who he had known absolutely was telling the truth. The punk's mind was a quivering, open book to him.

Afterward Chuck had let the punks go, although to a certain extent it was against his better judgment. But he couldn't think of a single good reason to hold on to them, and one very good reason to ditch them—namely, they made him sick.

Chuck was picking up a general feeling in the air—one of menace. One of danger all around, but he couldn't lock onto it. So he ordered the security men to start checking out all the buildings along the street, to try to find some indication of break-in.

But why? Why in the world would Wonder be here? What would draw him here?

He checked out one building but couldn't find any way in. Everything was padlocked, and there was one small hole nearby one window. Large enough for some kids to crawl through, but certainly not enough to accommodate the considerable bulk (not to mention fragile body) of Wes Wonder.

Over here.

Chuck glanced in Rommel's direction. The large German shepherd was indicating the building just in front of him—as large and run-down as the rest, but . . .

In here. Something's wrong in here.

Rommel's scenting ability was only average. As he had once crustily informed Chuck, if he wanted a tracker, he could try mindlinking with a bloodhound. But he was sensitive—even more so than Chuck—to imminent danger and, even more precisely, danger as posed by extremely nasty breeds of humans. It was a knack that Chuck had never had cause to question, and indeed had frequent cause to thank.

With Rommel's word on the matter a given, Chuck lost no time. Rather than waste minutes searching for means of entrance, Chuck simply formed a telekinetic fist and punched in the nearest boarded-over window. Wood splintered and it sounded like a rifle shot echoing up and down the street. The security guards reacted to it as if suddenly afraid they were under fire.

Chuck jumped in through the window and Rommel followed quickly. Chuck looked around and keyed into the same waves Rommel was picking up. Something was definitely wrong in this building.

He bolted up the steps, and his foot went through a weakened board. He stumbled and fell against the railing, and the banister almost gave out under him. He turned back to Rommel and said quickly, "Stay down here. Stuff's rickety enough as it is. If we both get injured, we're screwed."

Okay, Rommel said, slinking back down the stairs. *But watch yourself.*

"Why, Rommel, you care."

It's past my mealtime.

Chuck sighed and, after extracting his foot from the hole, started up the stairs once more.

He made it to the top and was greeted with the stench of odor and rot, of decaying bodies and human waste.

And he saw the body against the wall.

Wes Wonder, his clothes in tatters, blood covering every visible part of his body. He had been strung up against the wall with barbed wire that was tearing farther into his skin. The wire was anchored to the wall with huge nails.

"Oh, my God," gasped out Chuck, his horror blotting out the warning his mind was screaming at him.

And the Snapper descended from above.

He'd been clinging to the rafters and now he dropped down, hurling Chuck to the ground. The others were hurtling downward now as well, like batshit, hitting the floor in crouches.

Chuck was on his back, looking up as the foul-breathed creature over him brought a rusted knife down. Chuck moved his head just barely enough, and the knife slammed down into the floor next to him.

From downstairs Rommel started to bark furiously, and Chuck heard a thudding. Rommel was coming up the stairs, not especially taking care about rotted planks.

The Snapper on top of him heard it too, and automatically his head turned in the direction of the sound. Chuck took the opportunity to grab the Snapper's ear and twist his head around. Then, with a quick upraised pivot from the waist, he hurled the drug addict off.

He rolled to his feet and the others came in quickly. Too many, too fast. He reached entirely on instinct. He grabbed the outstretched hand of the closest one, trying to fight down the bubbling fury as he looked again at the bloodied body of Wes Wonder. He spun and hurled the Snapper as hard as he could into the wall. Then two were on him, shoving him back, and he grabbed the forearm of one of them, yanking it up and back as fast as he could. There was a resounding snap, and the Snapper didn't even notice it, but was simply aware that abruptly he couldn't hold on anymore.

Chuck bent over, grabbed the other one by the ankles, and then straightened up quickly. An unorthodox move, but effective, and the man slid over Chuck's back and crashed into the ground headfirst.

The others were charging toward him and then Rommel exploded into the room.

"Rommel! Don't kill!" shouted Chuck, but a shade too slowly as Rommel hurtled across the room and took down the nearest Snapper, iron jaws around the human's throat. Blood spurted and some flew so high that it struck Wes in the face.

Wes blinked. His breath rattled in his chest.

"Christ," said Chuck, who never used the Lord's name in vain. He started toward Wes and reacted automatically to the Snapper who tried to broadside him. One moment Chuck had been there and the next he wasn't, and the

Snapper saw the wall and only had time to think, in some befuddled way, "Oh, there's something in front of me," and then he hit it with such force that he dented the plaster several inches and left a round head-shaped imprint.

Chuck turned in time to see Rommel backing up, his muzzle covered with blood, roaring like a wild animal. God in heaven, that's what he was, wasn't he?

"Rommel, no killing!" shouted Chuck.

Rommel glanced his way, his thoughts a black cloud. *Should have fed me,* he said.

The remaining three Snappers came at Chuck, and in doing so, killed themselves. Had they left, Chuck could have devoted his full attention to holding Rommel back. But when they distracted him, they were dead but just hadn't realized it.

Rommel, freed of Chuck's locking grip on his mind, lunged toward the attackers. He grabbed one by the leg and the Snapper started to scream. Rommel backed up, dragging the Snapper kicking and howling toward the door. The German shepherd growled and snarled as the Snapper kicked at him, trying to shove the animal away. He managed to catch Rommel in the side of the head, which infuriated the great beast. Freed of the dog's grip, the man tried to crawl away and Rommel leaped forward, landing with his full weight on the man's back. His spine snapped instantly, and he was dead from the neck down. The last thing he felt was a pair of teeth clamping onto the back of his head, and then he was dead from the neck up as well.

Chuck, meantime, was gripped from behind by a Snapper with extraordinary strength. Chuck knew he was doubt-lessly being pumped up by some additional drug. He heard the man giggling dementedly in his ear, and Chuck's neck creaked. The other man was punching Chuck in the stomach, and Chuck decided he'd had more than enough of this treatment. Mentally he hurled back the man who was slugging him. The Snapper staggered, trying to pull himself together, and then he heard the warning growl. He turned, saw the infuriated Rommel, and ran straight for a window. The window was boarded over. It didn't slow him down as, propelled by pure terror, the Snapper smashed through the rotting planks.

It was, at best, a Pyrrhic victory, as the Snapper sailed headfirst toward the ground below. When he landed he did not get up again.

Still being choked, Chuck found the pressure points in his opponent's arm and shoved. The Snapper hadn't even realized that his hold had been broken before Chuck spun to face him. Quickly the Snapper attacked, but Chuck was ready, catching the arm and pivoting, hurling the Snapper away—

Straight toward Wes Wonder. Chuck had lost track of their position, and before he could do anything, the Snapper smashed into the cruel barbed wire that was imprisoning Wonder. He gagged and choked, barbs now protruding from his neck. Chuck, with a quick yank of his mind, pulled the man off, but that hardly helped. He fell to the ground, bleeding from a dozen vicious tears in his throat and upper body. He never even heard Chuck whisper, "I'm sorry."

Don't be, Rommel told him.

"Not now, Rommel," Chuck said tiredly. He stepped over the body of the Snapper and, using his TK, broke the barbed wire bonds that were holding Wes Wonder in place. Again without touching them, he carefully disengaged them from Wes's skin. The old man was a bleeding mass of cuts. It was nothing short of a miracle that he was alive at all.

Then again, miracles were his specialty.

Wonder slumped forward and Chuck caught him in his arm. The old man looked up at him, confused. And he whispered to Chuck, "It's not . . . Moby's fault . . ."

"It's not?" said Chuck in confusion.

"He . . . tried . . . to save me . . . but they didn't see him . . ."

Then his head slumped forward and his eyes closed. He was still breathing, but it was very shallow and already it sounded as if fluid was collecting in his lungs.

"Oh, God," and it was a prayer from Chuck as he hoisted the old man into his arms. Despite Wonder's apparent bulk,

Chuck was surprised at the relative lightness of him. "Come on, Rommel."

And suddenly both of them were alerted. Their minds screamed at them, of danger everywhere, and only seconds after that were the sounds of gunfire.

Now what?

"I don't know," said Chuck quickly. "You think . . . ?"

Complex?

"Got to be. Got to be the Complex. And . . ." Then he felt it even more, that singular presence. "Beutel. Beutel's here somewhere."

He was shouting to hear himself over the sounds of bullets flying. Still carrying the unmoving body of Wes Wonder, he ran to the window that the Snapper had so graciously opened for them.

One look told it all. There were the security guards, pinned down and heavily outnumbered, by the men whom Chuck had come to think of as the faceless men. Men in dark suits, with dark glasses. No army men this time. Clearly there was to be no military involvement with this one. For whatever reason, the decision had been made to let the Complex, with their own men, handle matters. Certainly their men were formidable enough.

The security men were crouching behind their cars or firing from within buildings. Chuck grimaced as he saw them being picked off, one by one. There was no chance of surrender being offered here. Someone—the president?—had taken off the kid gloves.

Then he spotted Beutel. Over behind an overturned and burnt-out old shell of a car. And at that moment, Beutel spotted him too. The assassin shouted and pointed, calling attention to Chuck's position, and Chuck cursed himself out as he ducked back inside. A bullet from a high-powered rifle chipped off a piece of board.

Nice move, Ace, said Rommel.

"Dry up, Rommel. Let's go."

He ducked down and made his way back across the room and out the door. In front of him was the stairwell leading both upward and back down.

Suddenly he heard the door being kicked in downstairs. That would seem to settle it.

He started up the stairs and looked down as he did so. Faceless men were ascending the stairs, pointing and shouting.

"Psi-Man says fall," Chuck murmured icily.

He reached out with a clenched mental fist and slammed down on the stairway. Barely held together as it was, it was all the additional push that was required to send the entire thing collapsing. The faceless men fell, screaming and twisting, to the ground floor below.

Nice.

Chuck wasn't too sure if he was happy about doing something that actually pleased Rommel. It probably didn't reflect too well on Chuck.

He ran up the stairs, Rommel following him, trying to be as careful as he could. Now not only did the stairs have to support his weight, but also the weight of the burden he was carrying.

He heard the sounds of noise and confusion, the angry yelling, and Beutel's voice float up to him from the ground floor. The normally laconic-sounding assassin was cursing fluently.

I remember him, said Rommel. *I wonder if his other hand tastes as bad as the one I tore off.*

"You're not going to find out," Chuck informed him.

Rommel grunted noncommittally.

They went up and up, as high as they could, and then Chuck forced open a heavy metal door that blocked their path. Air rushed in at him.

"It's the roof," said Chuck.

You were expecting the basement?

Sarcasm from a German shepherd was not a fun thing to have to put up with. Neither was being perforated, and if the faceless men found another way up, that's exactly what Chuck would be.

He stepped out onto the roof, Rommel right behind him.

A bullet cracked just over his head. He spun and dropped

to the ground, just in time to see a faceless man on the roof across from him. Rommel stood there, barking.

"Get down, blast it!" shouted Chuck, and Rommel hit the roof. A bullet whizzed just past where he'd been.

Chuck reached out, not having to see the rifle to get the feel of it. The force of his mind was like a tangible thing, and it snaked out and around the weapon. He yanked forward as hard as he could in order to rip the rifle from the man's hands.

The man refused to let go, which ultimately proved to be an error. For Chuck, since he was keeping his head down, couldn't be as precise as he would have liked to be. The agent held on so firmly that when the rifle went over the edge of the roof, so did the man.

Within an instant he was dangling over the alleyway. Chuck, not yet realizing that the man was still attached, released the rifle, and the first hint he had was the man's scream as he plummeted toward the sidewalk. Realizing instantly what had happened, Chuck reached out again and slowed the man, but it wasn't fast enough. The last thing to go through the faceless man's mind was his shoes.

Chuck felt nauseated.

You don't have time for that, Rommel informed him.

Sure enough, there was a pounding from the other side of the heavy iron door that led onto the roof. Somehow they had managed to circumvent the difficulty of the fallen stairway. Chuck looked around, trying to figure some way out. "Rommel! Check the street!"

Rommel ran to the edge of the roof and glanced over. An instant later he was chased back by gunfire. He looked testily at Chuck. *Now I see why you had me check instead of you.*

Chuck wasn't listening. His mind was racing, trying to come up with something.

The door burst open. Chuck spun and there was a man there with a gun aimed straight at him. Chuck mentally slammed the door back in the man's face, and there was a muffled yell from within and the sound of bodies falling. The stairway at that point was so narrow that they must have been standing single file and had gone down like dominoes.

He kept the door shut, focusing his TK ability on it, and now someone was pushing back from within. Beutel? Possibly. It was taking everything Chuck had to keep the blasted door closed, and he wasn't going to be able to maintain it forever.

The pounding, dammit, the pounding. And the air swirling around him, the noise . . .

Look up, Rommel informed him.

Chuck did so and couldn't believe he'd been so distracted that it had virtually managed to sneak up on him. A helicopter was approaching, coming in quickly.

He was dead, Chuck knew. It was taking his full concentration to keep the door shut. If he turned his attention from it to deal with the helicopter, the men would burst onto the roof and fill him with more holes than a badly plotted movie. But he was utterly exposed on the roof, and they could easily riddle him with bullets from there. Besides, how was he supposed to stop the helicopter? Kill the motor? He probably could—and send more men to the their deaths. God, the killing, the bloodshed . . . when was it going to end? When?

Now. That's all. It was going to end now.

Do something, Rommel said.

The copter loomed closer. "There's nothing I can do," Chuck said.

Great attitude.

Chuck braced himself, waiting for the hail of bullets. He still kept the door shut, out of reflex and maybe out of spite. If he was going to die, at least it wasn't going to be that bastard Beutel who brought him down. He'd deprive him of that pleasure at least.

There was no bullets, and moments later the chopper was hovering right over them. Chuck looked up.

The side door had been opened and a large basket, more than large enough to accommodate a man, was being lowered. And Chuck saw, peering through the door, Wyatt Wonder.

"Oh, my God," said Chuck.

Are we dead yet?

"No! Rommel, come on!"

The copter had gotten as low to the roof as it could, but there was no certainty that the decaying structure was strong enough to support a full touchdown and the pilot was clearly not taking any chances.

The moment the basket was low enough, Chuck shoved Wes Wonder into it. The basket was immediately hoisted back up and, even as it was, a ladder was rolled down. Chuck started to climb it quickly, hand over hand.

Move it, said Rommel, waiting impatiently.

There was the sound of repeated gunfire, and holes started appearing in the door. Chuck's head was splitting as it was. He couldn't hold them back much longer. Besides, holding the door closed wasn't going to make much difference if bullets flying through it managed to find their mark.

Chuck moved briskly and had almost reached the copter.

What about me?! demanded Rommel.

Chuck turned, glanced at the door, looked down at Rommel, and knew it was going to have to be a very fast move.

He clambered up the last rungs, hauled himself in with Wonder's help, but didn't stop to exchange so much as a word. Instead he mentally reached out and yanked Rommel into the air.

As he did so his grip relaxed on the door and it blew outward, agents of the Complex pouring out onto the roof. They were firing blindly, firing at anything, but fortunately they were buffeted back by the intense wind of the copter's blades.

Beutel hadn't emerged yet and Chuck was thankful for small favors. He pulled as hard as he could, not caring about how it looked so long as it worked. Rommel sailed upward and through the door of the helicopter, landing hard on the floor and tumbling out of control to crash into the far side of the loading bay.

"All aboard! Get us out of here!" shouted Wonder. He was wearing a flak jacket and goggles. "Move!"

The helicopter rose quickly and Chuck looked down. He saw Beutel emerge onto the roof and see the copter. Even from the distance, Chuck could see he was furious.

Suddenly the chopper lurched precipitously. "What's happening?!" demanded Wonder.

"The air's gone nuts!" the pilot called. "The currents are—"

"It's Beutel," said Chuck with certainty.

"Strafe the roof," Wyatt Wonder ordered.

"No!" Chuck countermanded him quickly. "Don't! If he sees barrels of machine guns he'll twist them or something. Blow them up, maybe even the copter."

"Well, what the hell would you suggest?!" snapped Wonder.

The copter was swinging wildly, buffeted by the winds that the psionic power of Beutel was calling up. Beutel was running across the roof as fast as he could, shouting orders, telling the faceless men to take aim.

Chuck reached out and yanked down Beutel's pants.

They dropped to around his ankles and Beutel, who had been sprinting, fell flat on his face, losing his concentration.

The winds immediately ceased and the copter shot upward at full speed. By the time Beutel was able to pull himself together, the redness of mortification coloring his cheeks, the copter was well out of range.

"Cute," observed Wonder.

"Sometimes the simplest methods are the best," said Chuck. "But they'll be after us."

"I know."

"They'll head straight to Wonderworld. Perhaps even bring more men."

"I know," said Wonder, but by now he wasn't paying attention. He was crouching over the basket that his father was lying in. Wyatt had had the foresight to bring along a medical team, and they immediately started working on him, shoving tubes down his throat, stanching the bleeding, and trying to repair the massive damage that had been perpetrated on him. In addition to the cuts there were numerous bruises, and Chuck shook his head sadly.

He didn't think the old man was going to make it.

And he was going to be right.

14

QUINT ALMOST SMILED.

When he heard the outraged voice of Beutel, and the incident related to him of how Simon had escaped, he actually felt a slight tugging at the edges of his mouth, unaccustomed as that was. Beutel was still shouting over the phone and Quint had barely paid any attention, picturing in his mind instead the marvelous image of Beutel facedown on the roof, his pants around his ankles, pounding in frustration as Simon sailed off into the wild blue yonder.

"I've had it with that bastard!" Beutel was snarling. "And no more of this pussyfooting around. I need access to full Complex troops. I want to invade Wonderworld and flush the son of a bitch out!"

"Invade Wonderworld?" Quint stroked his chin thoughtfully. "A fairly large undertaking."

"We've got the men. We've got the technology. All I want from you, Quint, is the go-ahead."

"I understand that Wonder has a command center a mile underground. Are you actually going to try and get to the command center?"

"Yes. But failing that, I'll hit the park itself. Their piddlyshit security measures won't mean squat to a full invasion. I'll have my men flooding down Main Street by crack of dawn if you give the go. And you know Simon. If people are being slaughtered topside, he's not going to just huddle under the ground. Especially if he thinks he's the reason it's all happening."

"And isn't he?" asked Quint neutrally. "What about getting Wyatt Wonder?"

"I don't give two shits about Wyatt Wonder, and neither do you. Anyone who keeps goosing our asshole-in-chief is fine in my book. If he lives or dies is of no interest to me, but dammit, I want Simon's head. I owe him. I owe him for what that monster of his did to my arm, and you owe him too."

Quint pondered it a moment, and then said, "Hold on." He put Beutel on hold, then switched to another line and dialed quickly. It was a direct line and moments later a familiar, and somewhat chilling, individual picked up the line with a brisk "Yes."

"Terwilliger, this is Quint. Our field man's best recommendation is that we do whatever we have to do to get the dangerous individual known as Psi-Man."

There was an impressed whistle on the other end. "Your field man is very ambitious," was the slow response, because they both knew without speaking damning words just what was being requested. "Is he aware of the difficulty of the campaign he wishes to mount?"

"He is indeed."

"Can he, in your opinion, pull it off?"

"I don't know," said Quint honestly. "All things equal, I'd say yes. But certain individuals have certain tricks up their sleeves."

"Yes, I would imagine they do." Terwilliger paused, considering. "The military could not be involved."

"Understood."

"An overt military strike would involve the president, and as much as we want to get Psi-Man, we do not wish to involve the president. Also, if the military is brought into it, the joint chiefs will start demanding to know what happened. To involve the military means to issue traceable orders, and I do not wish anything traceable."

"Understood."

"This would have to be entirely under the initiative of the Complex. If asked about it, I could neither confirm nor deny it."

"Understood."

Again Terwilliger paused, considering all the options.

"Do what you have to."

"Understood."

The line clicked off and Quint switched back to Beutel. "You still there?"

"Yeah, I'm still here, but this hanging around is beginning to burn my biscuits."

"The President's man is under the impression that the real reason you're going in is to nail Wyatt Wonder. Mine is that you're going in after Psi-Man."

"So?"

"So see if you can get them both and make everyone happy. And, Beutel . . ."

"Yeah?"

"I know about the history between you two, but if it's at all possible, I still want Psi-Man alive. Clear?"

"Clear," said Beutel, who gamely prepared to ignore the order.

"You have my authorization to full access of Complex facilities in the greater Los Angeles area. I'll contact Jenkins out there and so inform him. You'll be in charge of one of the biggest mobilizations of Complex manpower in history. And, Beutel . . ."

"Yeah?"

"Don't fuck up."

15

CHUCK STARED THROUGH a large window that opened onto a hospital bed. On the other side of the window he could see Wes Wonder, hooked up to a very impressive array of machines. On a nearby monitor were devices monitoring his various body functions, and although Chuck was certainly no doctor, he could see from the wavering trace lines that virtually everything within the old man's body was breaking down. He had simply been subjected to far too much shock and trauma.

Sitting next to Wes was his son, Wyatt. Wyatt could have been carved from granite. His hands rested on his lap, fingers clasped, like a small boy at school waiting oh-so-politely to be called on by the teacher. There was no one else in the room. Various medics had wanted to stay within, to keep working zealously on the unmoving form of Wes Wonder. But Wyatt had ordered them out, and since this was, after all, Wyatt's facility, deep beneath the bustling park known as Wonderworld, the medtechs had no choice but to obey instructions.

A soft hand fell upon Chuck's shoulder and he turned. Connie smiled at him. "You did your best," she said softly.

"I know. What galls me is when my best isn't good

enough." He leaned against the window, studying the tableau before him. "How did Beutel know?" he said in confusion. "How the devil did he know where we were? That Wes had made a break for it?"

Connie was silent for a moment, and then said, "I told him."

Slowly Chuck turned, looking at her incredulously. "What?" he said in a harsh whisper. "What are you saying?"

Connie didn't appear the least bit perturbed. "Oh, not Beutel, per se. A couple of his spies, or agents, or something. They threatened me in the park. They were . . . very persuasive. After it happened, I went immediately to Wyatt. That's when he decided to head up an air rescue." She leaned against the window, acting very nonchalant. "The old studio. Wyatt hadn't thought about it in years. It never occurred to him that that was where his father was going. Wes isn't going to make it, is he. If he had a hope in hell, Wyatt wouldn't have ordered everyone out of the room."

"Wait a minute." Chuck was still working on what she had said before, as calmly as if announcing the weather. "A couple of spies from the Complex were on the grounds?"

"Hmmm? Oh . . . yes. Disguised as blind people with special contacts, so the retina scanners wouldn't work. And they remained in communication with their masters via a disguised radar sighter."

"And—and after they got the information from you, they just let you go?"

She didn't say anything, and Chuck took her by the arms and stared at her. "Look . . . Connie . . . don't take this wrong. But you should be dead. I mean . . . these people are ruthlessly efficient. I can't believe they just let you walk away."

"They tried," she said softly. "They thought they had. But . . . they were wrong."

He shook his head in amazement. He was getting from her that same steady impression of nothingness that could only indicate someone who was utterly at peace. She wasn't lying. He was sure of it. "Then you don't know how lucky you are."

"Oh, I have an idea of it." She turned back to look once again at Wes. "He's dying."

"Yes," said Chuck. Why bother to try to put a gloss on something that obvious?

"I wonder what that's like. Dying."

"We all find out, sooner or later," he said.

"Yes," she said noncommittally. "Yes, I suppose we do."

Wes stared up unseeing. And then, slowly, his cracked lips moved and he murmured, "Moby?"

Wyatt slid his chair forward and took his father's hand. "Moby isn't here, Dad. He couldn't make it. But he's all right. I swear he is."

Wes slowly turned his eyes toward Wyatt, but he wasn't seeing him. "Of course he is. He's a cartoon."

Wyatt regarded his father for a moment. It was as if the light that had always somehow surrounded Wes was fading before his eyes. "Dad . . . it's me. Wyatt."

"I know it's you, Wyatt."

"I'm here."

"Where else would you be?"

"Dad . . ." He squeezed his father's hand. "Dad . . . I want you to know . . . everything I did . . . I did for you."

Wes coughed, an ugly, rattling cough, and yet he managed to half prop himself up. *"It wasn't what I wanted,"* he gasped out. "You had to remold the dream in your own image!"

"Dad!" Wyatt was pale.

"I had to pretend you weren't . . . that nothing was . . . because of everything you did. It's not my dream anymore. It's not what I would have done at all. All I ever wanted was the stars. You wanted the galaxy."

Wyatt's lip was trembling. To all others he was the invincible businessman, the keeper of the flame and the maker of the magic. But to this withered, dying old fossil,

he was nothing. He was garbage. He was the screw-up, the
rapist of the imagination, the one who took and didn't give.
The ugly, distorting mirror of the pure image of Wonder.

The father of Wes Wonder had gone to his deathbed and
died withholding approval of his son. And now, Wyatt
realized, it would happen again. All these years, Wes had
nursed his hatred and loathing of all that Wyatt had done.
That everything was such a tremendous success obviously
didn't matter to Wes. It was not the success *he* would have
made, not the company *he* built. It was this colossus that his
son had made, huge beyond imagining, omnivorous, om-
nipotent.

He thought he had done it all for his father, and yet now
he realized that that was a lie. He had done it for himself,
only himself. And his father knew this and loathed it.

Loathed him.

And now he was going to punish him, curse him with his
dying breath.

The old man's hand twisted around Wyatt's fingers. His
body trembled and then, in a low, guttural whisper, he
said . . .

"Good job, boy."

The words escaped him as if the last bit of air from a
deflating balloon. His body stopped trembling and sagged,
and a relieved sigh wafted from him.

And that was all.

Wyatt smiled, and leaning forward, he touched the old
man's knuckles to his forehead. "Thanks, Dad," he said to
the corpse in front of him.

And that was when the alarm sounded.

The first strike force of the Complex had made its run on
the entrances to the vehicle ports. All-terrain vehicles—
ATVs—had sped forward, mounted guns on either side
firing steadily. There were two dozen ATVs barreling
toward each of the four entrances, gates A through D, each
ATV manned by a single agent of the Complex. They wore
kevlar for protection, and jumpsuits over those. They were
making certain not to wear anything that could remotely be

mistaken for military. That was the order, as curious as that might sound.

Security headquarters, informed of the attack, immediately gave orders to close all the gates. The ATVs hurtled toward the gates, to be met by concentrated fire from security guards. There was furious fighting at all four points, and guards were hurled back, bullets stitching their way across their chests. But there were backups who returned the fire, strafing the ATVs and delaying them long enough for the massive gate doors to come together and slam shut, effectively sealing them off from the outside world. At Gate D, one of the ATVs almost made it through, for even though it had been hit broadside by a blast from an RBG 30, it skidded and lodged in between the doors as they slid toward each other. The driver, wedged in, tried to unbuckle himself and leap out of his vehicle, but he didn't quite make it before the doors slammed shut on his vehicle and, not coincidentally, him too. His scream was abbreviated and pretty much drowned out by the awesome clanging of the shutting doors.

The problem was that the attack on vehicle gates A through D were merely a distraction. After all, even if they had managed to get through, the access to the mile-below headquarters of Wyatt Wonder was quite simply impossible if you weren't authorized. They could have lobbed bombs at him, but the effectiveness would have been impossible to determine. If they had managed to access the elevators, certainly there were override systems that would have prevented the descent. Climb hand over hand down the shaft? For an entire mile? And be sitting ducks for whatever security measures Wonder had lurking within the accessway? Not bloody likely.

No, the true assault was at the main gate of the park itself, taking place mere seconds before the distracting attack. For at that main gate, Reuel Beutel, also wearing kevlar body armor and a jumpsuit, was rapping politely on the window of one of the cashiers. She looked at him and smiled, unaware of the attack that was about to be launched. "Yes?"

"Me and my friends would like admission, please?" he said.

"Certainly, sir. How many of there are you?"

"Oh . . . couple hundred."

She blanched at that and then he added, "But you're going to let us in free. You see . . . we've got invitations."

He held up his machine pistol and grinned. "Now don't hit an alarm or anything."

Quickly she stepped on a silent alarm. Beutel caught the motion of her foot. "Told you not to," he remonstrated her, and fired once. The girl was hurled back against the inside of her booth and slid to the ground, her nicely pressed white blouse with the duck insignia now covered with an ugly red splotch.

He shrugged. "Kids. They never listen."

That was when the alarm sounded, and Beutel and his men now charged the gates.

Beutel normally disdained guns, but for an operation of this size he was more than willing to make an exception. Besides, he had to admit there was something nice about wielding a serious piece of hardware like the weapon he was carrying. Yes indeed, very serious.

They were trying to slide the gates shut to cut off their access. Beutel reached out with his hand and created a block of pure psychic energy, keeping the doors jammed open.

It wasn't easy. He was fighting unseen grinding gears of machinery. But he wasn't going to give in and he stood there, his body trembling with concentration, as other agents ran past him toward the open gate. The man in first had the pressure bar out and set up within seconds—wedged in horizontally between the two open sides of the gate, it attached on either side with a superadhesive that caused almost immediate bonding. The gateway was now opened to welcome all comers, and men streamed in, driving ATVs or single motorcycles or on foot.

Their orders were quite simple: to cause as much mayhem as possible. The purpose of the mayhem was to flush out Wyatt Wonder and an unknown individual (of whom they'd all seen pictures) who would more than likely be accompanied by a large dog. Extreme caution was to be used at all times, and casualties were to be kept to a minimum. But there was the general understanding that if people wandered into the way of bullets, no tears were to be shed.

The moment the bar was in place Beutel released his psionic door stopper and took a breath. Even for a psionic of his ability, it had been a difficult task. Simon would have had an easier time of it.

Beutel winced at the memory. Simon. Chuck Simon. Psi-Man. He'd grown to hate the name, curse it in his waking and sleeping hours. At one time, Beutel had been the top psychic assassin for the Complex . . . indeed, pretty much the only one. He had been able to say or do exactly as he pleased. The psych reports that stated that he was mentally unstable . . . well, hell, he'd been able to pretty much ignore them. Because he was the only game in town, and he knew it and so did they.

But then Simon had come along. The fair-haired boy. The nice guy with psionic power that tested out even stronger than Beutel's. Beutel had been furious, galled, and even more so when they had teamed up Simon with that goddamned mongrel. For Beutel's one weakness was an almost pathological fear of dogs, and the combination of Psi-Man and the hound from hell had been too much even for Beutel to cope with.

But he had coped, hadn't he. Framed Simon for murder and then put him in a position where his only course was to go on the run. Trouble is, Beutel had been certain that Simon would have been laid low by now. The damned Quaker had been most uncooperative on that point. Not only had Simon survived, but his mangy sidekick had actually robbed Beutel of his right hand.

Reflexively he looked down at what had replaced it. It gleamed in the artificial light shining down from the dome overhead.

Somewhere below ground, Simon was hiding. He had to be brought up.

All around Beutel, people were running, screaming in confusion. The orders were to watch civilians whenever possible.

Beutel turned and shot down a family of four with one quick burst, and watched them die. Then he turned in a slow circle, shouting, "Psi-Man! That was just the beginning! Come out! And bring Wonder with you!"

Upon hearing the alarm, Chuck immediately turned toward Connie . . . except she wasn't there. He realized that he'd been so fascinated watching the scene between Wes and Wyatt—perhaps even being something of a voyeur, but he wasn't going to berate himself over that now—that he hadn't noticed Connie's quiet departure. Where had she gone off to?

Wyatt now emerged quickly from the room, looking right and left as already men were running past him, wielding weapons. "What's going on?" demanded Chuck.

"Major invasion. Come on."

He started running and Chuck had to double his pace just to keep up with him. As he did so he sent out a mental command for Rommel to join him. "Your father . . . ?"

"He's dead."

"Oh." Even though he was running, Chuck felt he should say something. "I'm sorry . . ."

"He's dead and I'm going to take care of him." He sounded distracted even as he spoke, as if his mind were back with his father and not on the current state of emergency at all. "All he wanted were the stars."

"Wyatt?"

"In here."

They entered a larger room than Chuck had ever been in before, and it was overwhelming. It seemed almost the size of a football field. Three huge screens ringed the upper half of the room, and on them were alternating shots of men with guns everywhere, everywhere throughout the park. They were shooting at anything that wasn't moving, strafing the fronts of buildings, tearing up lampposts, destroying signs, hurling millions of dollars' worth of Wonder merchandise into the streets and trashing it. Everywhere, everywhere was hysteria. People were being wounded and trampled in the melee. There was nowhere to go, nowhere to run, nothing to do but to die. The sounds of screaming, screaming everywhere filled the room.

"Turn it down, for pity's sake!" shouted Wyatt, and the sounds of terror dropped to an acceptable level.

The room was completely packed with smaller monitors, and control consoles, and Chuck immediately knew what the place was—it was the command center for all of Wonderworld. All the aspects of park operation were monitored from this central place.

Wyatt strode through and people kept running up to him, hurling facts and figures at him. Wyatt was above it all, literally. As if in a dream, he said, "The president's really gone over, hasn't he. All right then."

He went straight to the nearest computer console and spoke into the microphone, "Computer, voice ID."

"ID confirmed as Wyatt Wonder," the computer said crisply.

"Go to defensive code Omega. Defensive code Omega."

One of the men standing nearest him looked up in surprise. "I never heard of that."

"You didn't design the computer," replied Wyatt. He turned and pointed to two security guards. "You and you. Come with me. We have a job to do. A tribute to my father."

Chuck stared at him in amazement. "Wyatt, for pity's sake! You're under attack! I understand your state of mind, but don't you think whatever tribute you have in mind can wait?"

"No, Chuck . . . it can't," said Wyatt simply. "But you stay here and on the screen you can witness . . . a true sense of Wonder." He walked out, followed by two puzzled but obedient guards.

Chuck looked back up at the screens. Obviously there were cameras set up throughout Wonderworld, and they were cutting from scene to scene.

Then he heard a voice and saw a familiar face. There was

Beutel, screaming Chuck's name and, oh, my God, he just shot some poor young man who had fallen to the ground, writhing and grabbing his leg.

"No," whispered Chuck, "don't."

And Beutel stood there on the screen, screaming again, "I want you, Psi-Man!" and he stomped his foot down on the boy's back and shot him in the head.

Chuck turned, bolted for the door, and two guards interceded. "Don't go out there, Mr. Simon," one of them said. "It's suicide."

"He's killing people! They all are!"

"Mr. Wonder has it in hand."

"Mr. Wonder is thinking about tributes to his father!" snapped Chuck, and turned back to the screen pointing, "and that madman is . . ."

He stopped, his eyes widening. The screens had cut to another shot. And there, in the middle of the crowd, looking for someplace to run to, was Connie. There was a glimpse of the area behind her. She was near the castle.

"My God!"

Even the guard reacted to that. "Isn't that Miss Lopez?"

Chuck didn't answer. He charged toward the door and when the guard tried to stop him, Chuck mentally shoved him out of the way. The guard tumbled to the side, totally confused and looking around for what had hit him. By the time he recovered, Chuck was gone.

Chuck thundered down the hallway, arms and legs pumping. He sensed, rather than saw, Rommel falling into pace behind him.

What's going on?

"Beutel," said Chuck quickly. "Leading a massacre upstairs."

How many men?

"Don't know. Looks like hundreds."

Dinnertime.

And Chuck, even after seeing the ruthlessness that had been gong on upstairs, knew in his heart that he couldn't allow Rommel to do as he wished. But he didn't say it.

* * *

Wyatt stood above the body of his father, his face set. The guards were on either side, looking at each other for some clue as to what was supposed to happen now.

"Mr. Wonder . . . ?" one of them asked cautiously.

"Lift him off the bed, put him on that gurney," said Wyatt, without looking at them. "Then follow me."

"But . . . sir . . . the invasion topside . . . maybe we should . . ."

"Wonderland," said Wyatt crisply, "can take care of itself."

16

THE OMEGA DEFENSE kicked into gear as the central computer sent messages to all parts of Wonderworld. Harmless rides and features designed to bring only joy and amusement were reprogrammed, given new data and new imperatives. Emergency traps long prepared were triggered.

The Safest Place on Earth, within two minutes' time, became the deadliest.

In Imagineland, an agent stopped briefly to glance at an especially alluring display of flowers. He knew that he was supposed to be trashing everything he saw, but these were particularly lovely. They reminded him of a type of flower that grew back home.

He took a step forward to sniff them.

It never occurred to him that in a moment of whimsy Wyatt Wonder had made sure that all the flower pistils were actually pistols. Consequently, it took him completely by surprise when the pistil took aim and blew a third nostril in his nose. He staggered back, already dead, and the flowers opened fire on other agents who were standing nearby. Special bullets spewed out and they were laughing at the kevlar armor as they went through.

It was poetic justice of sorts. So many times had clumsy gardeners accidentally mowed down flowers. Now the flowers were getting to do the mowing down.

Agents came running in response to the barrage and hurled grenades at the flower beds. The flowers exploded and the firing stopped, and the agents thought that their troubles were over. They thought this for about two seconds, and then the herd of unicorns burst forth from the Unicorn Petting Zoo. The wonders of Animagic worked their spell once more as the unicorns stampeded down upon the agents. Some men died beneath the thundering hooves, while others were gored horribly on horns that, in myth, had marvelous restorative and healing powers.

Agents spun, not knowing where to look first, and several leaped into their ATVs and gunned them, determined to get out of there. Unfortunately Animagic gremlins had been busy, and when the agents started to roll forward, their super-high density, unbreakable tires fell off, hurling them ignominiously to the ground. At least they had only a few moments to be embarrassed about it before harpies descended, gleaming claws bared, and began to rip them to pieces.

One agent, whose weapon had been lost to the unicorn stampede, was being pursued by a particularly fierce-looking harpy that was emitting the most bloodcurdling shrieks he'd ever heard. Off to his left was a mass of fleeing civilians, and he thought he'd be safe if he could only get to them. He shoved his way in, joining the mob of terrified people, and even started screaming with them in order to blend in. He was safe, certainly. He had to be. Whatever insane creations Wonder was hurling at them, they couldn't possibly be smart enough to discern friend from foe. There was no way they could conceivably be able to distinguish the park attackers from helpless park-goers.

It was a comforting thought, an erroneous thought, and as it so happened, his last, as the talons of the harpy closed over his head and carried him off, leaving the people around him unharmed.

*   *   *

In Pioneerland, arrows were raining down upon the confused agents. Everywhere men were falling with evil-looking shafts sticking out of them, shafts that again had the incredible knack of not hitting anyone except the park's attackers.

One agent sought refuge inside the Big Ol' Bear Animagic show, in which life-size bears in funny clothes danced and cavorted for the amusement of the patrons. But as he came in the bears were just leaving, lumbering toward the exit door as their internal programming was retooled and given new imbearatives. The agent didn't know that, though, and when he saw the ludicrously dressed grizzly lumbering toward him, a guitar under his arm, he actually smiled. The grizzly swung the guitar around, aimed, and fired. The first blast hurled several of the agent's major internal organs across the room, and the second blast hurled the agent after them. At least he died amused.

The bears smashed through the doors and out into the streets, looking around for victims. Several agents in ATVs barreled toward the united bears, which was a mistake. The bullets from the ATVs' weaponry ripped through the bears' tough skin, and one of the bears even went down, but the rest knocked aside the ATVs or lifted them over their heads and hurled them back down again, stomping on them with their considerable weight until the flesh of the men was hopelessly mingled with the metal of their vehicles

One agent almost escaped. He was confronted by a very small Kodiak bear cub who seemed harmless, until the Kodiak cub shot him in the head with his whimsically labeled Kodiak camera.

In Spaceland, the Martians attacked. They were small and green and extremely deadly, firing short staccato laser blasts into the confused agents. The agents fired back, but for the Martians their strength was in numbers. It seemed that for every single Martian that was reduced to quivering piles of scrap, another two sprang into place.

The "Super Scary Space Monster" ride came to life. A

tribute to every B-movie vision of space, the monsters staggered out of their comfortable home into the streets of Wonderworld, tearing into every agent they saw. One agent fired and kept firing on one especially huge monster with jaws the size of a bulldozer. It didn't slow the creature down, and the thing scooped the agent up and hurled him into his mouth. The huge maw closed and chewed him up thoroughly before spitting him out. The Animagic creation did not, after all, *really* have a digestive system. That would have been silly.

To the creatures right, giant crab monsters were crushing agents between their massive claws.

Agents were breaking and running as their weapons barely slowed down the mechanical babies of Wyatt Wonder. Several agents ran into the "World of Outer Space" display that normally gave customers the feeling that they were in deep space by providing eerie music, an unending field of stars, and an incredible feeling of weightlessness. When the agents entered, however, it added one more thing to the mix—a vacuum. Within seconds the air had rushed from their bodies and the men exploded. Ironically one of them, just before he died, was recalling how as a child he'd wanted to be an astronaut when he grew up so that he could leave his footprints on a distant planet. As it turned out he got to leave an entire foot, which came to rest on a mockup of Neptune.

The things that went on in Joyland, the adults-only section of the park, were absolutely unspeakable. Suffice to say that the loudest screams came from there.

Beutel didn't know where to look first.

The whole joyful raid had fallen completely apart. All around him his men were dying. The thing had turned into a catastrophe.

He was standing just outside the entrance to Pioneerland. He turned just as one of the once-cheerful grizzlies descended toward him with incredible speed. If it had been a real bear, Beutel might have had a problem since his power worked erratically against organic objects. But this was a machine—incredibly sophisticated, but a machine nevertheless. Beutel's power snaked out and sent the creature's legs exploding from either side of its body. It tumbled to the ground and tried to drag itself forward toward its intended victim using its massive forepaws.

Beutel flexed his metal hand, which was attached to his metal arm. Although Rommel had ripped off only Beutel's hand at the wrist, the entire arm couldn't be saved by the time Beutel managed to get help and be brought to the nearest Complex medical facility. Indeed, Beutel had lost so much blood that it was a miracle he was alive at all. But his pure fury had kept him alive, and when he'd been told that an entire mechanical arm would be added to replace the one he'd lost, he was almost glad. The strength provided by such a weapon was a tremendous plus, and he was looking forward to using it against Simon at his earliest opportunity.

He even had the scenario planned. Using the arm's superior strength, he would ram the thing right into Simon's chest, then rip out his heart and make him watch it as he died. Over and over again he had imagined himself driving that fearsome arm home.

For now he practiced on the bear, smashing the arm down into the chest of the thrashing animal, using his TK to keep the sharp claws at bay. He wrapped his hand around an assortment of mechanical guts and then pulled. His arm got stuck for a moment, tangled in the metal innards. Well, certainly that wouldn't be a problem with the far more yielding internal organs of Chuck Simon. Within a few moments Beutel had yanked the arm free and was holding a satisfying collection of micro-circuitry. The bear stopped moving.

Suddenly Beutel sensed him.

He turned and looked around quickly and spotted Chuck, who was looking in the other direction. Chuck had obviously sensed him as well and was trying to find him. But the air was filled with confusion and the screams of the dying, and it was hard to lock onto him. Beutel had spotted him so quickly largely out of luck.

Then, above the melee, he heard a woman scream Simon's name. A dark-haired woman, Mexican, and she was shouting again in Simon's direction. Chuck was turning, trying to spot her.

Perfect. Perfect. Things were going his way after all.

Chuck, after finding Rommel below ground, had made for the elevator and shot quickly up to the surface. Rommel had been less than enthused by the thought of hurling themselves into the insanity that was breaking out overhead, but Chuck was determined. Rommel wondered for the umpteenth time why he put up with this sentimental human drivel even as the elevator disgorged its passengers.

Chuck ran out of the castle just in time to have an agent stagger up to him. The agent, to his credit, actually recognized Chuck, his eyes widening, and he tried to bring his gun around to shoot him. But then the last of his strength gave out and the gun slipped from his nerveless fingers. He feel forward and lay still, the arrow in his back finally finishing him off.

Chuck ran, Rommel right behind him. He chose the direction that looked as if it would give him the angle that he'd seen the castle from when Connie had been in the picture. It took him into Pioneerland.

He passed the graveyard that was situated directly outside the Haunted House. An agent had taken refuge behind a tombstone there and when he saw Chuck and Rommel run past, he took dead aim with his machine pistol. He would have had them too had not skeletal arms with bits of dead meat on them ripped up from the grave beneath his feet. He screamed once and only once as he was dragged down beneath the ground.

Chuck, unaware of his close call, stopped running and turned, trying to locate Connie. To get her the hell out of there. What had she been doing there anyway? She had probably just wanted to go up to the park. Simple and harmless as that. She hadn't known that they would be under attack shortly. She'd probably been upset watching Wyatt with his father. Maybe even tremendously uncomfortable—perhaps she didn't like seeing her all-powerful boss in such a vulnerable state of mind. So she had fled to the relative simplicity and safety of a park that had now gone wild.

In the distance on Main Street, the Animagic cartoon characters of Wonderworld were doing their job. Moby Duck, in his quackers personna, was ripping through the agents. He was holding one in each hand, crushing each with his four powerful fingers. Doofy had commandeered an ATV and, just like in the short, was driving like a lunatic, running over any agent who stood in his way. Wall-Eyed Pike was slamming his atomic-powered pike— the spear kind, not the fish kind—through the front and back and front of two agents who'd had the misfortune to be standing back-to-back at the time. Pistol Pete, cursing in colorful cartoon-language nonprofanity, was just simply shooting right and left seemingly randomly, but actually with tremendous accuracy.

Cartoon characters gone berserk. Every child's nightmare.

Chuck suddenly became alert as Beutel's presence announced itself. Psionics could always sense when another of their kind was around. The question was where, in this seething and panicking mass of humanity, was the murdering bastard?

Chuck heard his name screamed and he turned. There was Connie. My God, what a miracle. He started toward her, separated from her by a wall of hysterical humanity.

And suddenly an equally solid wall of pure wind hit Connie and hurled her off in another direction. Chuck saw her yanked away, as if by invisible strings, and it took him a second to react. A second too long, and then she was in the arms of Beutel.

Beutel put an immediate choke hold across her neck and held a machine pistol up to her head. His expression was deadly, his intention clear.

"How good are you, Psi-Man!" he howled, laughing above the din. "Good enough to get the gun away from me without my shooting her first? Good enough to kill me, huh? Make my brains leak out of my ears? How good, Psi-Man? How good?"

Kill him, said Rommel.

Chuck froze, sorely wanting to. "There's got to be another way."

There isn't.

And then Beutel was moving.

He dragged Connie along as if she weighed nothing and Chuck paced him, never taking his eyes from him. His mind raced. If he tried to use his power, Beutel would know and kill her before Chuck could stop him. The assassin was quick that way.

And his hand . . . what had happened to his hand. The hand that was holding the machine pistol was some sort of gleaming metal.

An agent ran past Chuck, screaming, batting at his neck. Two small chipmunks, one wearing a fedora and leather jacket, the other a loud Hawaiian shirt, were clamped onto his throat, ripping it out with their large teeth and chittering away hysterically.

Chuck shoved him out of the way and then realized he'd lost sight of Beutel and Connie . . .

No. There they were. Climbing into the flume ride.

"Leave the dog behind, Psi-Man!" Beutel was shouting. "And come on along or else when we get to the end of the line, it's the end of the line for her!"

The huge fake log in which they were seated started to move, water splashing around it. There were two more logs attached directly to it and Chuck ran as fast as he could. Rommel was right behind him, and Chuck leaped into the last log just as the lead one, with Beutel and Connie in it, had vanished into the darkness of the ride.

"Rommel, stay!" shouted Chuck.

Rommel gave the ride a quick glance, saw the water, saw that this was definitely a high-speed ride. *No argument here.*

Then Chuck descended into the darkness as well.

The flume moved faster and faster. Chuck heard screams ahead of him, which was natural for this kind of ride. But here they took on an entirely different meaning as Chuck envisioned Beutel performing all sorts of hideous tortures upon the helpless Connie. He started climbing over the seats, crouching low, clutching on for dear life as the flume hurtled forward. Water hurled up around either side of him and he kept his head low because the ceiling was low. If he wasn't careful, he'd have a crewcut down to his neck.

"Having *fun*, Psi-Man?" Beutel's laughing voice came from the darkness ahead. "I just looooove roller coasters, don't you?"

In point of fact, Chuck hated them. But he didn't think about it. He thought only about the desperate girl ahead of him, who needed him.

He got to the front end of the log and paused, trying to muster the nerve to jump to the next one. He was given some help when the flume suddenly hit a major dropoff and Chuck, crouching, was hurled forward. He tumbled into the next log, cracking his head against a seat railing.

The combination of the darkness and velocity and the impact all gave Chuck a sense of vertigo. The world spun around him and it was everything he could do to hang on and not be hurled from the ride. What were the rules? Don't stand up? Don't ride not belted in? Don't, for pity's sake, try to climb to another car? God, were there any other rules he could ignore?

He scrambled forward and then for a moment they burst out into light.

There. Right in front of him. Beutel had climbed back to meet him and was drawing back that metal fist of his.

Then they were hurled back into darkness. Chuck blocked where he thought the blow would come from and sure enough, there it was.   .

The darkness held little fear for Chuck. He had lived in darkness during the chaos in Colorado. He swept the arm past him and, using Beutel's own momentum shoved him back. Beutel fell, cursing, and Chuck was suddenly hurled forward, staggering, by another sudden lurch in the flume ride.

Beutel brought his foot up and it impacted with Chuck's crotch.

Chuck went down, moaning, pain rocketing through him faster than the flume. Beutel lashed out again, his foot catching Chuck in the side of the head. Chuck was knocked onto his back and Beutel lunged toward him.

Chuck only had a split instant to focus and he did so, hurling Beutel back with the power of his mind. Beutel stumbled and the flume dropped off again, sending Beutel tumbling back into the lead log.

The flume lunged right and then left and Chuck did everything he could just to hold on. Then the flume began to slow down and, moments later, burst into the light and stopped.

Chuck looked up and Beutel was just hauling Connie out of the log. Chuck, for his part, was still giving up dry heaves from getting kicked in the balls.

Beutel brought the machine pistol around and fired.

An instant before he did, Chuck leaped out of the log, landing on the far side in the water. Huge pieces of the log were blown out, sending shards and chips all around him. He covered his head and tried to reach out, unseeing, to locate the gun, reasoning that if it was firing at him, then it couldn't be aimed at Connie.

Then the hail of bullets ceased, and Chuck, not wanting to take any chances, recalled his mental probe. And now Beutel wasn't there. He could sense it. Chuck raised his head, dripping, and peered over the log. Beutel was in the distance, dragging Connie toward the castle that was the best-known landmark of Wonderworld. Its tall, gleaming spires shone there, including the tower in the middle that was the highest and proudest, that seemed to symbolize everything that was good and powerful and strong in Wonderworld.

Beutel risked a glance down Main Street. He saw his men being torn to shreds by oversize cartoon characters. It did not exactly fill his heart with cheer. This was going to look extremely bad on his report. But if he could nail Simon . . .

He howled as Connie clamped her teeth down on his forearm. Furiously he smashed her on the side of the head with the gun butt and she yelped. He was curious to notice that there was no blood from her.

He glanced back. Simon was right behind him.

To his immediate left were steps leading up the castle. That was where he headed, dragging the screaming Connie with him. And right on his heels came Psi-Man.

17

WYATT WONDER WALKED slowly around the gleaming chamber into which, after an elevator ride in an elevator neither guard had known existed until now, he had placed his father. The chamber was decorated with Wonderana, memorabilia stretching back decades. There was the first Moby Duck wristwatch. There was a program book from the opening day of Wonderworld. There was a complete—absolutely complete—library of every single Wonder film ever made.

And there was his father, inside a shining casket. Wyatt stood next to him for a moment, placing his hands on it.

"You wanted the stars, Dad. It would be cruel not to give them to you."

He stepped back and said in a loud voice, "Computer. Initiate ignition cycle."

"Cycle activated," said the computer primly. "Five minutes to ignition."

"Good," said Wyatt softly, and then repeated, "good."

He stepped out of the chamber and the door cycled shut behind him.

All was silent for a long moment.

Then Moby Duck waddled across the chamber and leaned against the transparent casket. He smiled.

"We sure gave 'em a run for their money, didn't we, Wes."

The spiral stairs seemed to curve up forever. Beutel dragged Connie up and up, and every time she started to slow he goaded her with the machine pistol. He heard Simon pounding up the stairs behind.

Beutel wasn't sure where he was going but somehow felt that he would know. He would know when he got there.

Higher and higher. Yes, that was it. Of course. Simon had a problem with heights. Advantage to Beutel. Game and match.

They got to the top of the stairs and a rope was hanging there with the sign, "Off limits." Beutel yanked the rope out of the way and kept climbing. He felt as if he were in an old-time swashbuckler.

"Please," gasped Connie, yanking on his arm, "we're not supposed to be up here."

"Shut up," he snapped, not in the mood for her nonsense.

Now the stairs stopped and there was another obstacle, a door that read, "Keep out." This one meant business. So did Beutel. He blasted it open with the force of his mind.

They emerged into the open air, onto a flat area—not exactly a roof, since this was not the highest point of the castle. But what served as a roof nonetheless. Around them on all sides were turrents and battlements and, dead center of the roof, a tall, gleaming main tower. It stretched high, glittering in the artificial sunlight, seeming to wait for some knight to scale its unclimbable sides.

Beutel ran along the edge of the roof, which was bracketed by the ramparts. He climbed up onto a rampart and looked down at the dizzying drop.

And that was how Chuck found them.

"Beutel!" screamed Chuck. "Let her go! This isn't about her!"

The woman started to struggle in his grasp. She was

rapidly starting to become a nuisance. Up on the rampart, Beutel's eyes gleamed and he said, "Sure, Chuck. For old times' sake."

He spun and flung her off the rampart, toward the ground below.

"No!" screamed Chuck, and reached out to try to stop her fall, focusing entirely on her.

He was certain that, at that moment, Beutel would turn and shoot him to pieces. It never occurred to him that Beutel would shoot Connie.

But that's what he did. He fired on her and her body twisted in midair, supported there by Chuck's TK power. She howled Chuck's name as the bullets ripped her to pieces.

Horrified, he released her and she plummeted. He knew that Beutel wouldn't have missed. He knew, he could tell from the sounds of the bullets impacting, that indeed Beutel hadn't.

The ground would be a mercy to her.

For Beutel, there was no mercy.

Chuck hurled a TK blast that shattered the rampart where Beutel was standing. Beutel leaped over it as pieces of brick hurled all around him and he opened fire on Chuck, laughing madly.

Chuck staggered back, not even realizing that he was hit as his mind ripped the gun from Beutel's hand and twisted it into a pretzel shape. He started toward Beutel and only then felt the warmth of his own blood running down his arm.

Wind suddenly whipped around Chuck, hurling him about like a leaf in a storm. He staggered, buffeted, and Beutel came in fast and smashed Chuck in his wounded left shoulder. Pain exploded behind Chuck's eyes.

"You're dead, Psi-Man," grunted Beutel.

He grunted again and this time Chuck blocked it with his good arm, sending the impact past him, and then stepped forward quickly and hurled Beutel back. He turned his TK on Beutel, like a giant fist, encompassing the assassin and starting to crush him. Connie's image appeared in front of him, pushing him on, reminding him of what this man was all about. Reminding him of the cold-blooded murderer that he was about to extinguish as Beutel felt massive pressure on his torso, his ribs about to collapse and penetrate his lungs and heart . . .

Rommel would be proud of him, he knew.

Which was why he eased up.

The moment Beutel felt the pressure lighten he threw a blast of power at Chuck. Chuck was lifted off his feet and slammed against the side of the main, gleaming tower in the middle of the roof. He pulled himself up, using the massive tower for support, and couldn't help but notice the gentle vibration of the tower that seemed to be more pronounced with every moment.

Beutel came at him fast, too fast, and drove a snap kick into Chuck's stomach. Chuck went down, gasping, already weakened by blood loss.

Beutel clamped onto Chuck's throat with his cybernetic hand. Chuck gasped, trying to find TK power to drive Beutel back and Beutel was blocking Chuck's efforts with his own. Their minds were like two rapiers engaged, riposting and blocking.

And neither man noticed that, high above their heads, the top of the great dome over Wonderworld was—for the first time that anyone could recall—irising open.

Wes Wonder sat up, leaving his body behind, and smiled at Moby. "Yeah, we sure did, buddy," he said, and stepped down, feeling better than he had in years.

Moby glanced around. "Nice place. So . . . what'd you say to your kid?"

"What he wanted to hear."

"And how'd you know what he wanted to hear?"

"Because"—smiled Wes—"it was what I wanted to hear when my father died. Old reprobate."

Suddenly Moby frowned. "Say . . . Wes . . . just what exactly *is* this place, anyway?"

"A parting gift from Wyatt, I believe," said Wes slowly. "Yes . . . I do believe that's what it is."

"Parting for whom?"

"For us, Moby," and Wes gestured, taking in the entire area. "All for us."

Outside, from a safe distance, Wyatt watched the power build up with pride. Everything was going smoothly. The new technology that had been developed, specifically for the Wonderstar One, would keep damage levels down to a minimum. Oh, certainly the castle would be destroyed—but that was minor. A small price to pay indeed, for giving his father the stars.

Perhaps . . . yes, he would leave the castle that way. In rubble. So that when people would see it, the questions would be asked, and the stories spread, and the legend would grow. Yes indeed, people should know. And they would.

In less than two minutes, they would know.

Chuck slipped in under Beutel's guard and, with his mind, lifted the assassin over his head and slammed him headfirst into the tower. Beutel groaned and fell to the floor, holding his head and then snarling.

If Chuck had been of a mind to, he could have bashed in Beutel's skull. If he'd had more strength, he could have hurled him off the roof. But he had neither. He was still leaning against the curiously vibrating tower, and his head was splitting.

And now Beutel was in front of him, drawing back that massive metal fist.

"Waited a long time for this, Psi-Man," he said, and drove it toward Chuck's chest with every ounce of strength he had.

Chuck pivoted, barely dodging, and Beutel's fist, his entire arm, smashed into the tower. So great was the arm mechanism's strength that Beutel sank in up to his shoulder.

The arm smashed into delicate circuitry within the tower, the impact ripping open some wiring in Beutel's arm, Normally it would not have been a problem. Beutel would simply have withdrawn it and, even with the minor damage, would still have been in more than sound working order. He would have been ready to try again, and this time would probably have fulfilled his dearest wish of ripping out Chuck Simon's heart.

The internal computer of the tower reported a disruption of some circuitry. Plus a breach of the hull. But it was nothing that couldn't be repaired. Lines were immediately rerouted, taking all power from the area of the breach and sending it elsewhere. An automatic hull sealant, another Wonder breakthrough—a kind of living metal, really, to accommodate stray bits of deep-space matter that might penetrate the hull—seeped in to repair the breech instantaneously.

Beutel tried to pull his arm out and couldn't.

"What the fuck?" he muttered, and yanked again, giving it everything he had.

Except he didn't have anything. Power to his arm was dead. And something was holding it in place.

"This isn't funny," he muttered, and then more loudly, "this isn't funny! Dammit! Let go, you stupid tower!"

He pulled as hard as he could. He even backed it up with his TK power. But he might as well have not been pulling at all.

Chuck staggered away and now the entire roof was shaking.

Beutel's eyes went wide with horror as a faint possibility occurred to him of just what he was armpit-deep in. "Simon!" he screamed. "Help me! *Simon*!"

Chuck was a witness. He should do something. He had to.

He yanked on Beutel, adding his own psionic power to Beutel's, but it didn't make a damned bit of difference. And then the roof was shaking so violently that he couldn't even stand up. And from far, far below, beneath the bowels of the castle, there was a rumbling.

"Holy shit!" howled Beutel, knowing beyond all doubt. "It's a rocket! *It's a goddamn rocket! Simon! Do something!*"

Chuck did something. He got the hell out of there.

He staggered to the rampart, leaving a trail of blood and Beutel's screams behind him, and hurled himself over the battlement. He used his last bit of TK power, pushing against the ground to slow his own descent. Still the ground came up at him with horrible speed and he had barely slowed himself down enough before he hit.

He was next to Connie.

She was lying there, filled with holes, unmoving. His voice sobbed in his throat as pieces of the castle were falling all around him.

She stared at him . . . and winked.

He looked back in amazement.

Of course. She was dead. And now he must be dead. They were together in death. Moronic, but nice.

And at that moment, Rommel ran up between them.

Chuck looked up in surprise and said, "Rommel! You're dead too?"

Humans, sighed Rommel. *Come on.*

He dragged himself up, wrapping an arm around Rommel's great neck. "Connie," he gasped. "Connie . . ."

Rommel grabbed the back of her blouse with his teeth and moved quickly . . . as quickly as he could considering he was pulling the weight of two people—one with his jaws, the other just hanging on for dear life.

The castle collapsed faster and faster and Rommel moved with more speed than he would have thought possible. He dragged Chuck and Connie the length of Main Street.

Behind them, the great tower started to lift off.

Beutel's screams were drowned by the roar of the rocket's mighty engines as it took off with a roar of fire and exhaust. A very compact roar, to be sure, else it wouldn't have mattered if Rommel had dragged them out into the parking lot, it still wouldn't have been far enough. But it was all part of that ever-present Wonder Magic.

The castle collapsed completely as Wyatt Wonder's final, long-planned tribute to his father hurled skyward. Realizing that they were now a safe distance, Rommel stopped dragging them and Chuck turned to watch the rocket soar upward, up toward a hole that had magically opened in the great dome. The noise was deafening, but the accuracy was pinpoint. It was the most majestic thing that Chuck had ever seen.

And just before the rocket vanished from view, he was quite certain he saw a small, struggling form, as small as a gnat, near the top of the rocket, pounding and writhing. Then they were both gone and the noise of the rocket grew fainter and fainter, although Chuck's ears were still ringing.

That was when Rommel remembered. *What happened to Beutel?*

"Oh," said Chuck. "He spaced out."

Chuck turned and glanced at Connie's unmoving body . . . the beautiful face that he had been hallucinating only moments before had actually winked at him.

She winked again.

He looked down at her, really looked.

There were the gaping holes in her chest that Beutel's bullet had torn. And there, sizzling and smoking, was burnt circuitry.

She cleared her throat.

"Chuck," she said, "I think there's something you should know . . ."

18

"SHE WAS UNAWARE," Wyatt Wonder told him.

Chuck was standing there, in the Animagic workroom, watching the animagicians put Connie Lopez back together again. Rommel was looking on in amazement.

"How—how could she not know that she wasn't real?" said Chuck.

"Did you know?"

"Well . . . no . . . but . . ."

"You had sex with her. Some very enthusiastic sex with her, judging by the condition of your room."

Chuck's lips thinned. "Was she programmed for that too?"

"She was programmed to be a real woman," said Wyatt patiently. "What she chose to do was her own affair . . . pardon the expression. I made her to work in Joyland but, frankly, got somewhat fond of her. So I kept working on her to make her more and more sophisticated . . . although there are some holdovers from her original Joyland use. For example, she can secrete a fairly strong, hormone-inducing scent from between her legs. For most people, it's subliminal."

"But dogs would pick up on it immediately," said Chuck slowly, looking at Rommel.

Rommel merely said, *Told you.*

"As I said, most of the time she was unaware of her true nature. You see, Chuck . . . I wanted her to enjoy life. How can you really enjoy life if you know you can never really die. It automatically separates you from humanity." He looked at her fondly. "Of course, if someone makes an attempt on her life, her backups kick in and she becomes aware. Some agents tried to poison her and after it didn't work, she alerted us to their presence. And once she hit the street and was still alive, she also realized again. But like the other times, I'll wipe her memory of it. Haze it over. She'll be fine."

"Chuck," she murmured.

He came over to her and she said softly, "I'd still like to go with you."

He couldn't believe he hadn't realized. She'd never . . . seemed . . . right to him, but the explanation had never occurred to him. Still . . .

"Ohhhh," he said slowly, "Connie . . . I don't think it'll work out. I mean . . . you know. I'm a Quaker. You're an android. If there's kids, we won't know which way to raise them. You know how it is."

"Of course." She smiled. "I know. Chuck . . . I love you."

He returned the smile. "I love you too, Connie."

One of the Animagicians said, "Okay, shut her down. Give her cells time to recharge."

Connie's head slumped to one side, her eyes still open. Chuck passed a hand over her eyes to close them, then turned and walked away. Wyatt Wonder followed him.

They walked down the hallway as Chuck said, "She won't remember that, right? I mean . . . I lied to her. I hate for her to remember a lie."

"You are leaving then," said Wyatt.

"Yes."

"Looking for Haven?"

Chuck stopped and turned to Wyatt. "How do you know about that?"

"You asked me about it."

"Oh. Right. So I did."

"What is it, anyway?"

Chuck sighed. "Maybe nothing. A place I heard of. A place where there are supposedly lots of people like me. Psionics. A better place."

"Haven." Wyatt shrugged. "I'll keep my eyes and ears open. If I hear of anything, I'll find a way to contact you."

They reached the garage and there, glistening and shiny, sat the RAC 3000. Wyatt gestured and Chuck said, "Oh, I couldn't . . ."

"I insist," said Wyatt. "Oh . . . it's got a chameleon feature. Can give itself an entire paint job in a different color in ten minutes . . . just in case you want to make yourself that much harder to find. With my best wishes."

He stuck out a hand and Chuck shook it firmly. "Thank you, Wyatt," said Chuck.

Rommel had already climbed into the car. *Hey! There's about a dozen raw steaks in here!*

"Rommel thanks you too," he added.

"No problem," said Wyatt.

Chuck stepped into the car and Rac promptly said, "Welcome back, Mr. Simon. A pleasure to be working with you again. My bullet marks are repaired and I must say you are looking fit. The weather is . . ."

"I'll be surprised. Okay, Rac?"

"As you wish, Mr. Simon. Is there anything else I can help you with?"

"Yeah. Can you play some Barnes and Barnes music?"

"Rock and roll," said the car distastefully.

"Sort of. If you wouldn't mind . . ."

Mozart was piped into the car and Chuck sighed.

Good lunch, Rommel told him.

"I'm glad you like it, Rommel."

Wyatt shook his head. "Talking to a dog and a car. Isn't that the silliest thing you ever heard, Moby?"

Chuck regarded Wyatt curiously. "Who are you talking to?"

"Moby Duck. He's right here," and Wyatt pointed toward empty space. "Can't you see him?"

"Oh. Sure," said Chuck slowly, not sure whether Wyatt was joking and not sure he wanted to know.

He shut the door and rolled down the window as Wyatt leaned against the car and said, "And of course, you're welcome back here anytime. In fact, in three months will be our grand reopening."

Chuck shook his head slowly. "I hate to think of certain people in government knowing about all the carnage that went on and . . . I mean, wanting to kill you. And the president just gets away with it?"

"Well . . ." said Wyatt slowly, "I must admit, I'm not a good person to have angry with you. The president will have his difficulties, starting"—he glanced at his watch— "about now."

The president appeared on TV screens all over the country as a voice intoned, "Ladies and gentlemen . . . the President of the United States."

As was his custom, he walked to the center of the set, where a chair and desk awaited him. As he started to sit down and say, "My friends . . ." an extremely rude noise entered the living rooms on TV sets throughout the country.

Americans looked at each other. From one end of the country to another, children asked their parents, "Did the president just fart?"

The president didn't hear it. He sat there, talking, telling the people of how he had heard about the awful happenstance at America's safest place and that he was going to launch a personal investigation.

And over the entire speech, as the president grimaced in that way he had during speeches, his words were accompanied by constant and incessant sounds of flatulence. It went on for five minutes, louder and louder, the president oblivious, as all over the country people went into total hysterics. People called up neighbors to shout, "Are you watching?!" People rolled on the floor. Children wet themselves laughing. Adults wet themselves laughing.

Technicians on the broadcast were going insane. They heard it but couldn't figure out where it was coming from, couldn't cut the audio because no one had the authority to break off the president's speech like that. They checked every frequency, couldn't find anything.

No one had ever heard of a high-tech whoopee cushion that broadcast farts directly into the nearest television feed. It had never existed before. So no one knew that the president was sitting on one.

No one, of course, except Wyatt Wonder.

And somewhere, a duck was laughing hysterically.